SURRENDER

Haunting Emma

Lee Nichols

NEW YORK BERLIN LONDON SYDNEY

First published in the United States of America in December 2011
by Bloomsbury Books for Young Readers
www.bloomsburyteens.com

For information about permission to reproduce selections from this book, write to
Permissions, Bloomsbury BFYR, 175 Fifth Avenue, New York, New York 10010

Library of Congress Cataloging-in-Publication Data
Nichols, Lee.
Surrender / by Lee Nichols. — 1st U.S. ed.
p. cm.
Summary: Ghostkeeper Emma's mysterious visions are realized when she comes face to face with Neos, the ancient, repulsive old ghost that has haunted her, torn her family apart, turned her friends against her, and ruined minds and lives.
ISBN 978-1-59990-686-7 (hardcover) • ISBN 978-1-59990-423-8 (paperback)
[1. Ghosts—Fiction. 2. Supernatural—Fiction.] I. Title.
PZ7.N5412Sur 2011 [Fic]—dc22 2011006231

Book design by Nicole Gastonguay
Typeset by Westchester Book Composition
Printed in the U.S.A. by Quad/Graphics, Fairfield, Pennsylvania
2 4 6 8 10 9 7 5 3 1 (hardcover)
2 4 6 8 10 9 7 5 3 (paperback)

All papers used by Bloomsbury Publishing, Inc., are natural, recyclable products made from wood grown in well-managed forests. The manufacturing processes conform to the environmental regulations of the country of origin.

SURRENDER

We all gaped at Harry for a moment, despite the eerie whispering filling the room—then someone screamed. The sharp, high-pitched sound cut through the whispers and set my heart racing. Natalie and I exchanged a glance, and Lukas pushed his lunch aside, preparing for the worst.

"Who screamed?" I asked, my voice soft. "Where did it come from?"

"I don't know," Natalie said.

"Okay, if—" I didn't get any further, because the kids at the other tables abruptly rose from their seats. Chairs scraped the floor, and a sudden hush fell. They all stood with blank expressions on their faces, looking almost militaristic in their school uniforms.

"Crap," I said under my breath. "Crap, crap."

I've never liked bad boys. On TV shows, when the girl is torn between her sweet best guy friend—who is not-so-secretly in love with her—and the standoffish bad boy, I always root for the best friend.

But standing in Bennett's attic room, my arms twined around him, I finally saw the appeal. I shouldn't have been there. Shouldn't have let Bennett's drug-stained fingers stroke my neck, shouldn't have lied to Simon about him. And I definitely shouldn't have been kissing him when I was supposed to be downstairs with the rest of the team, trying to figure out Neos's next move.

Yet I barely protested when Bennett nibbled my neck. "I—I should—oh—"

He pinned me with his piercing blue eyes. "Yes?"

"Um . . ." I licked my lips. "I forgot what I was going to say."

"You don't have to say anything. Just keep making those little noises."

I let out a sound I didn't recognize as he traced my spine with his finger.

"Yeah, like that," he whispered.

Oh my God. How could I have been so wrong about bad boys? Forget the best friend, I wanted *this*—the unpredictable charm, the danger, the heat. Did anything else matter? I closed my eyes and ran my fingers through his hair in the spinning darkness—then stopped when I heard a cough from the doorway.

My eyes snapped open and I caught a glimpse of someone standing at the top of the attic stairs. It was Simon, peering inside.

"Simon!" I yelped. "Go away!"

"Emma . . . ," he said. There was something weird in his tone, something more than just *I've caught you with your drug-addled boyfriend who shouldn't be here.*

"What?" I asked. "What's happened?"

Before he answered, two people stepped into the room. Well-dressed, faintly familiar, and completely unamused.

And Bennett said, "Mom . . . Dad?"

I've always had moments when I wished I could yell "Freeze!" and the world would stop, giving me a chance to think of a great comeback line, retake a test, or cancel the inane grin I just flashed the guy I was crushing on. This was one of those moments. This was the *queen* of all those moments.

What were Bennett's parents doing here? Well, yes, it was their house, but did they have to show up this very minute? Why not an hour from now, when I'd be done with Bennett? Okay, I'd never be done with Bennett, but at least I might've been fully dressed. Instead I was wearing a lacy white tank top, which no parent would deem modest.

As I struggled into my sweater, my hand brushed Emma's ring, hanging on its chain around my neck. I considered whipping it on and disappearing in a cloud of ghostly embarrassment. On the plus side, it would end this terrifying encounter; on the minus side, I'd be deserting Bennett, which seemed really cowardly. And maybe turning into a ghost wasn't the best way to impress his parents. I mean, as much as I *could* impress them, given the whole making-out-with-their-son thing.

"I want you to meet Emma," he told them, as though there were nothing awkward happening. "You've probably heard a lot about her."

"Hi," I squeaked.

"It's all true," he said, with an easy grin.

His parents didn't smile back. They just stood there, radiating disapproval, which gave me ample time to discover that Bennett got his looks from his mom, who was dark-haired and beautiful. She had on an asymmetrical burgundy sweater over black fitted pants and low boots and wore her long hair slicked back in a ponytail. Carefully made up, her pursed lips caused the only apparent wrinkles. Bennett's eyes, though, came from his dad, who, aside from the blue marbles of brilliance under his furrowed brow, was almost completely gray, from his hair to his dress shirt and pants.

"The Sterns just got back from Europe," Simon said into the silence. "They arrived late last night."

Mr. Stern took a step toward Bennett. "What have you done to yourself?"

Mrs. Stern's gaze flicked from Bennett to me and back again. "This is worse than I thought. Much worse."

"So your flight was good?" Bennett said.

"You look like a—" His mother made a choking sound. "A ghost."

"A *junkie*," his father said.

"And these are my parents," Bennett told me. "John and Alexandra. They're very pleased to meet you."

Simon took pity on me. He motioned me toward him and said, "Emma, let's give the Sterns a few minutes alone."

Bennett squeezed me tight before letting go. I crossed the room, and Simon slipped me a twenty. "Go into town and get yourself a chai."

I turned back toward Bennett, unsure whether I should leave him, but he wouldn't look at me. His body was rigid with anger, and I decided I wasn't helping things by being there. I took the twenty and fled.

I found Natalie sitting by herself in the solarium off the kitchen. In front of her was a mug drained of coffee and a half-empty bowl of soggy cereal. The latest *Elle* lay open on the cushion beside her while she texted on Sara's hand-me-down Sidekick.

It was mid-December and the sky was radiant blue.

I knew the air outside would feel subzero, at least to this California girl, but the inside of the solarium was warm and tropical, the heat of the sun mixing with the scent of Anatole's lemon and orange trees.

Natalie glanced at me. "Your sweater's inside out."

I groaned and reversed my sweater. As I poked my head through the neck hole, I said, "Did you know Bennett's parents are here?"

Natalie stopped texting and frowned. "Really?"

"Have you met them?"

"Only once. They're kind of . . ."

"As frigid as the weather outside?" I suggested. "Even more stern than their son?"

"Yeah. It's weird how their last name fits them so well. It's like Stern is in their blood."

"So it's not just me? They're cold with everyone?"

"Wait, you were *just* with them? And your sweater was inside out, and—" She cackled and started furiously texting again. "You and Bennett were getting all *dirty*, and they walked in on you?!"

"'All dirty'? What does that even mean? And who are you texting?"

"Sara. She wants to meet for deets."

I sighed. "Fine. Tell her I'm buying. Higher Grounds in twenty minutes."

Natalie and I walked into the village, bundled in our wool coats and scarves, grumbling that we should've driven. The sun was shining, but a frozen wind whipped through the streets, stinging any exposed skin. I'd wanted to wear Bennett's sister's down jacket, which I'd been borrowing since the weather dropped below forty, but was afraid his parents would see me. Better to freeze. They already thought I was the slutty girlfriend who turned their son into an addict; I didn't need them thinking I was a petty thief, too.

"Where's Lukas?" I asked Natalie. "We should've invited him."

"He went home," she answered softly.

I stared at her. "You mean *home* home? I thought he was still fighting with his parents."

She shrugged. "It's three days 'til Christmas. He said he's never spent a Christmas away from them. He's giving it a chance, no matter what they think of him."

Christmas. I didn't want to think about it. My parents hadn't reappeared since they'd visited me in the hospital after I burned my hands on Coby's ghost. God, that still sounded ridiculous, even to me. Last Christmas, I'd been home in San Francisco with Max and them. We'd opened gifts in the morning, walked in Golden Gate Park, eaten roast beef and scalloped potatoes, played cards while finishing off a chocolate cheesecake, and fallen into bed.

My idea of a perfect Christmas.

This Christmas, I was living three thousand miles across the country, locked in an ongoing battle with an evil wraith master, and freezing my butt off. I didn't even know if my parents were coming.

Well, of course they were—that's what families *did*. But as much as I tried to convince myself they'd show for Christmas, I couldn't get over my doubts. I really needed them to be here—to make me believe Neos hadn't ruined everything in our lives, including my favorite holiday.

"God, can we walk faster?" I stomped my feet. "I think I've got frostbite."

"Race you!" Natalie said, knowing she'd win. Not that I cared, as I trailed behind her. It was working—I could feel my feet again.

We slid on a patch of ice, almost wiped out, and were giggling by the time we opened the door of the coffee shop. There was a comforting blast of warmth and java smells, the sound of the milk steamer, and old movie posters decorating the walls.

Sara wasn't there yet, so we ordered three skinny red-eye chais and watched Simon's twenty bucks quickly diminish. The fireplace nook was free, and we lounged in the ragged brown leather chairs, propping our feet on the brass grate next to the flames.

As I took my first sip of chai, I thought about Lukas and his parents. Would they be happy to see him? He deserved that—for them to love him, no matter who he was.

I knew my own parents loved me, even though they'd screwed up, first keeping my abilities as a ghost-keeper a secret from me, then disappearing entirely. They'd thought they were protecting me, and maybe they had for a little while. Still, I couldn't help wishing our lives were a little more normal. That we were worried about what to get each other for Christmas, not about Neos reappearing in a murderous rage.

"Do you miss your parents?" I asked Natalie. "If they lived closer, would you go see them?"

She swirled her chai, silent for a moment. "You don't get it," she finally said. "You think you do, but you don't. It's not like you and Lukas. They're not just crappy parents, they abused me. You don't miss that."

"I'm sorry." I leaned over to hug her. "I shouldn't have—"

"It's okay. Christmas just sucks, is all."

"It so does." At least this year it did. Aside from worrying my parents weren't coming, I'd accomplished nothing in the gift-giving department but a graphic novel for Lukas and a book of poetry for Simon. I had no idea what to get for Natalie, who was impossible to please, and Bennett, who had everything. And was I supposed to get something for Harry and Sara to stow in their castlelike mansions? "Totally sucks."

"What sucks?" Sara asked, coming up behind us.

"Christmas," I said, handing her a chai.

"Obviously," she said, taking a sip.

"*You* don't like Christmas?" Natalie asked.

"What's there to like? It's prefab sentiment, tacky lights, and a day when all your favorite restaurants and stores are closed. Plus your parents never get it right. You ask for the *Glee* box set and they get you *High School Musical*. And my sister is visiting with her husband—I hate him."

"I knew you were our friend for some reason," Natalie said.

"It's certainly not for that guy you hang out with." Sara glanced around the coffee shop. "Where is he, anyway?"

"If you mean Lukas, he went to make things right with his parents," I said.

Sara smiled softly. "He's kind of sweet."

"I thought you were still in love with Coby," Natalie said pointedly.

"And I thought you couldn't be with Lukas because you're both ghostkeepers," Sara replied, even more pointedly.

I was caught in the middle of all the pointiness. On the one hand, I wanted Sara to hook up with Lukas so she could let go of Coby's ghost. On the other, Natalie was my best friend, and I wanted her to have someone as cool as Lukas. She needed that in her life.

But she didn't need the complications that came with them both being ghostkeepers. Their powers were so different, I wasn't sure which of them would begin to lose their abilities. And I didn't want that to happen to either of them. You shouldn't have to give up something that makes you special just to be in a relationship.

"Life would be so much simpler if one of you fell for Harry," I said, wishing it were Natalie.

"Maybe he doesn't like either of us," Natalie said.

"Harry?" I said. "Have you met him? He'd take either of you in a—"

"Who cares about Harry?" Sara interrupted. "We're

talking about Lukas. And what if *he* doesn't like either of us? Maybe he's stupid enough to like Emma."

"Leave me out of this," I said. "I've got enough problems."

"He did make you that sheath for your dagger," Natalie reminded me.

"That's so cute," Sara cooed.

"Not to mention he's hotter than hot butter."

"*Dude*," Sara said, giving a nice impression of Lukas.

I shook my head. " 'Hotter than hot butter'—is that even a thing?"

"You heard it here first," Natalie said.

I drained my chai. "Do you think I should go back and see what happened to Bennett? Can your parents still ground you when you're twenty?" There had been serious tension in that room, and I worried about what was being said. Bennett had enough going on; he didn't need to be feuding with his parents.

"Ooh, tell me everything," Sara said, pulling her chair closer. "And stop hogging the fire."

"Take my seat." I stood and tossed my cup into the trash.

"You can't go yet," Sara protested. "I need details."

"There are no details," I told her. "They walked in on us kissing."

"She was naked," Natalie said.

"I was not!" I grabbed my coat and headed for the door. "Tell her the truth."

As I left, I heard Natalie say, "Basically, they hate her."

"No one hates Emma," Sara said. "Believe me, I've tried."

I didn't bother waiting to hear Natalie's answer,

because how could the Sterns *not* hate me? First I was responsible for their daughter's death, and now for their son's addiction to Asarum. If I were them, I'd hate me, too.

The air felt even chillier on the way home. Maybe it was the wind coming off the ocean, or maybe I was just anticipating the inevitable cold front from Bennett's parents. As I stomped through the pockets of ice on the museum's drive, I wondered why they'd suddenly returned.

Because they knew Bennett was hooked on Asarum? Because I was living in their house and they hated me? If they kicked me out, where would I go? Would Natalie come with me?

Inside, I shed my coat and went straight to Bennett's attic room. "It's me," I called, climbing the rickety steps.

He met me at the top and took my hand. "Are you all right?"

"I'm fine. I mean, slightly embarrassed, but otherwise . . ." I stopped at the look in his eyes. "What? What happened?"

He dropped my hand and turned away, and I took in the state of the room. His dresser drawers were ajar and a suitcase lay open on the bed. I recognized the pale blues and grays of his wardrobe, messily folded and half stuffed in his bag.

"No," I said. "*No.* You can't go."

He sat on the edge of the bed. "C'mere."

I crossed the room and stood between Bennett's legs,

looking down at him. I still felt a nervous shiver just being close to him, like the first time a guy you like kisses you—like the first time *he* had kissed me. Maybe I'd never get over that feeling, not with Bennett.

He traced a finger down my arm. "It's hard to think when you're this close."

"Then stop thinking."

"We need to talk."

"No, we don't," I said, and kissed him. I just wanted to go back to before his parents interrupted us, before he'd started packing. I didn't care that we might get caught again, I needed to recapture the feeling that we could be together. That everything would be all right. I'd gotten too used to his being here. I didn't think I could do this without him anymore.

I kissed him and he lay back, shoving his suitcase to the floor, running his hands over my body. He made me feel beautiful, like I was the only thing he ever dreamed about. I wanted to forget everything but the taste of his mouth and the way his hands made me feel. I'd never been this way with anyone else before—insatiably wanting and breathless. But I couldn't stop thinking about that suitcase. I pulled away.

"I'm going to miss that," he said, with his gorgeous smile. He traced a path along my hip, unwilling to let me go completely.

I leaned back into him, unable to resist. "Then why are you leaving me again?"

"They kicked me out, Em."

I frowned. "Your parents?"

"They told me to get off Asarum or go."

"So get off it!" As beautiful as his smile was, it would've been so much better if he stopped taking the herb that stained his fingers and killed his appetite. Plus, I wasn't convinced he ever slept anymore.

"I can't. Not yet. Not until Neos is dead."

I sat up on the bed. There was nothing to say about that; we'd already had the argument a dozen times. And I'd finally decided I had to trust that Bennett knew what he was doing. "How much do your parents hate me?"

His grin returned. "A lot."

"Then why are you smiling?"

"They're pissing me off, so I'm happy that you're pissing *them* off."

"Bennett, I don't want them to hate me." I didn't want to be left alone here with them, feeling responsible for their daughter's death and the defection of their only remaining child. I couldn't see how we would comfortably coexist.

He rolled over and pressed against me. "They don't know you, Emma. Once they do, they'll fall in love—like I did."

"But until then?"

He laid his head in my lap. "Just let me enjoy it."

We repacked his suitcase together. I never liked packing, but folding Bennett's worn shirts and fraying khakis felt intimate, meaningful—and I wanted to stay with him as long as I could.

"Where are you going?" I asked. "Back to your dorm?" I could live with that. His room at Harvard was only forty minutes away.

"No, I'm still on leave. You know they want Simon in charge of the Knell? Well, he wants me there to protect him."

"God knows he needs protecting." Simon's powers had never been strong, but what he lacked in strength, he made up for in knowledge. And I couldn't help thinking that he might persuade Bennett to kick the Asarum while they were both at the Knell—in fact, I wondered if that wasn't part of his plan. I knew better than to mention it, though. "Who put Simon in charge?"

"The few ghostkeepers who survived Neos's massacre."

I paused mid-fold, remembering that night. I felt lightheaded, still overwhelmed by the all the violence and the losses. "How were all those deaths explained? Neos's wraiths must have killed twenty people."

"There are ghostkeepers everywhere, Emma. The Knell's been sending low-powered ghostkeepers into police departments and the FBI for generations. The official report says a gas line exploded."

"They've got an answer for everything," I said, bitterly. "Maybe they should've come up with a way to stop Neos before any of this happened."

I still wasn't ready to forgive the way the Knell had treated me or my family. And now there were all those senseless deaths, including my poor aunt Rachel. It made me sick sometimes, how everyone who worked for them was so devoted. Including Bennett, Simon, and Natalie.

Bennett tossed a pair of socks into his suitcase without responding. He'd grown up with the Knell; he'd always be loyal to them. I used to worry he cared more about that ancient ghostkeeping society than he did me. It was an old argument he clearly didn't want to reopen, and I was starting to wonder if I could be wrong. If Bennett believed in them, there must be something good about them.

"It doesn't matter," I said. "Everything will change with Simon in charge. He deserves your protection. I'm glad it's you."

I tucked the last T-shirt into his suitcase. He flipped the lid closed, then rested one drug-stained hand on the back of my neck. "I don't want to leave you," he said.

I kissed his gaunt, beautiful face, not liking that I was getting used to the way his looks and scent had changed since he started taking Asarum. "I know," I said. "But you won't be gone forever."

And, I told myself, *he wouldn't be like this forever.* His body would fill out, his blue eyes that I loved so much would sparkle again, and that familiar, irresistible boy smell would come back. But with Simon's warnings about Asarum ringing in my head—how Bennett would eventually lose control—I only hoped I was right.

Simon was waiting downstairs, his suitcase packed. He was dressed in the camel-hair coat he'd first shown up in, and the sight of it made my heart break. I hadn't known him long, but he'd been an amazing guardian. He was smart and intuitive and, yeah, we got on his nerves, but he'd been there for us. I couldn't believe I was losing him along with Bennett. I threw myself at his chest, hugging him hard.

"I'm going to miss you so much. And I don't think I've ever said thank you."

"Bloody hell, Emma." Simon half grinned. "Stop, before you make me cry."

Natalie stormed into the foyer. "Bloody hell is right! What the fu—"

"Natalie!" I said, cutting her off. Not that I minded her swearing, but I knew the Sterns were around, and I didn't want them thinking any worse of us.

She strode to the front door and crossed her arms. "You can't go. Neither one of you. I won't let you."

"Natalie—" Bennett started.

"We're a team," she interrupted. "We need to stay together. You're letting them break us up."

"I *am* them now," Simon said. "I'm only doing what I think—"

"Emma needs you both," Natalie said. "You know Neos is coming back, and every time he comes back, he comes back stronger. I can't protect her—I can't even protect myself!—and I'll be damned if she gets hurt because she's worried about me, so no, you're not leaving. You're not going anywhere."

"Come here, my little Fury," Simon said.

Natalie crossed the hall to him, a stubborn glint in her eyes, and he spoke quietly to her. I wanted to go comfort her, but Bennett stopped me. "Let them talk."

"She *is* kind of like one of the Furies," I said. I knew from Latin classes they were goddesses of revenge.

"If anyone's a Fury, it's you," Bennett murmured back.

Before I could respond, I noticed the Sterns in the hallway that led to Mr. Stern's office. They stood there disapprovingly, eyeing the scene Natalie was making. She was taking this harder than I expected, and I wished Lukas was here to make a joke and ease the tension. After Simon comforted Natalie for another minute, Mrs. Stern cleared her throat.

Simon glanced at her and winced. "Ah, yes. One more thing."

"They're kicking us out?" Natalie asked.

"No, no," Simon said. "Quite the opposite. The Sterns have agreed to act as your guardians."

I glanced at them, thinking Simon should've added the word *reluctantly* somewhere in that sentence.

Natalie snorted. "Another day, another guardian."

"I know." Simon laid a hand on her shoulder. "You get tossed around a lot. And if it were anyone else, I'd worry. But you two will be okay."

Natalie sniffled some more, then pecked Simon on the cheek and crossed the room to fiercely hug Bennett. She gave the Sterns one last evil look, then ran upstairs in a burst of tears. Yikes. Not her most shining moment.

"Well, she's a bit high-strung," Mr. Stern said, disapproval in his low voice.

"How about this, Dad?" Bennett asked, his own voice a little too smooth. "You hold off judging Natalie until after you battle Neos a couple times, then we'll see what 'high-strung' is. She doesn't have half of Emma's power—hell, she's a *summoner*—and she's faced down a nightmare wraith master without flinching. Over and over again. You have no idea what we've been dealing with."

"Bennett," his mother said warningly.

"After Neos killed Olivia," Bennett told his father, "Natalie stood and fought—and so did Emma. What did *you* do?"

"Bennett!" his mother snapped.

"I mourned," his father said.

"Well, right, yes," Simon blurted, attempting to end

the tension. "We should be on our way. I'm sure Natalie will be just fine. She's got Emma to take care of her."

"But who's going to take care of Emma?" Bennett asked.

I leaned into him, standing as close to him as I could without actually touching him. I hated that we had an audience for our final moments together. Especially when that audience included his parents. I wished I could end all of this, fix things between Bennett and his parents, make everything right for Natalie, and stop Bennett from leaving. But I couldn't figure out how to do any of that.

"Just come back to me," I finally answered. "That's how you can take care of me."

"I promise," he said. Then he kissed me, a full-on everything-you've-got kiss, like he didn't care that his parents were standing ten feet away from us. And at that moment, neither did I.

I stayed in Bennett's room the rest of the afternoon. I didn't snoop through his drawers, but I did rifle through his old CDs, flip through the books on his shelf—half of them graphic novels, the other half college texts—and lie on his bed, staring at the timber-frame ceiling. Counting the cobwebs, aching for Bennett. Yeah, we were physically apart, but still totally together. After so many rough starts, things were actually good between us, and I wanted them to stay that way.

I tried to figure out what Neos's next move would be. Where he'd show up and what he'd want. If I finally dispelled Neos, everything would be okay. Bennett could stop taking Asarum, he and his parents could move on, and Natalie could stop worrying about how she was going to protect me.

Neos was no doubt hiding in the Beyond, licking his wounds, but I couldn't go there. He had the distinct advantage over me of being able to appear in both worlds. I was stuck here, waiting for him to find me, never knowing when he'd strike next.

I stayed in Bennett's room, contemplating my options, until it grew dark and I felt the first pangs of hunger. I couldn't stand to face the Sterns over the dinner table, so I slunk down to the kitchen to beg Anatole to make something for me and Natalie.

As I hovered in the kitchen doorway, the better to escape if the Sterns appeared, I suddenly missed Nicholas. Yeah, he'd betrayed us, but that didn't stop me caring about him. And Neos had fooled him into thinking he could bring back his sister. I understood that fierce desire to see someone you missed.

Plus, if Nicholas had still been here, he could've played lookout for me while I snuck some food. He would've liked that.

Anatole and Celeste were arguing over dishes in the kitchen. There were pots steaming on the stove and silver waiting to be polished on the counter. The sudden reappearance of the Sterns, their real employers, had thrown them into a tizzy, but they stopped when they caught sight of me.

I know you're busy, I said. *I'll just grab something for me and Natalie.*

Celeste gestured toward a tray on the marble counter. *I waz going to bring it up thiz moment.*

On the tray were two sandwiches, a chopped veggie salad, and two homemade chocolate truffles covered in cocoa powder. *Are those . . . peanut butter and jelly?* I asked, surprised Anatole even knew about such things.

He pursed his mouth. *I hear her in the hallway, making the noise. I want to cheer her up. I know she likes theez.*

I smiled. He and Natalie had a funny relationship. They were always swearing at each other in French, even though she couldn't hear him, but every now and then the fondness came through.

Looks délicieux, I said, grabbing the tray. Natalie wasn't the only one learning a little French around here. Thank you, Internet.

Emma, Celeste called after me. *You will like zem.*

Of course I will! And the truffles, too.

I mean Mr. and Mrs. Stern. Zey are kind.

I'm not worried about liking them, I said. *I'm worried about* them *liking* me.

I let the kitchen door swing closed behind me and carried the tray upstairs.

"Who is it?" Natalie croaked, when I knocked on the door.

"Me," I said. "I've got food."

She opened the door and blew her nose.

"Charming," I said. "Thank you for that." I set the tray of food on the desk. "It's been three hours since they left, how can you still be crying?"

"I stopped for a while," she answered. "Then started again. It's not like you haven't spent whole days in bed, wallowing."

"True." I handed her a plate. "Food helps."

She prodded the sandwich, then swiped some of the jam dripping from the sides and licked it off her finger. "Did you make these? Anatole usually guards his homemade strawberry jam with his life. Well . . . not his life, but you know what I mean."

"He made it for you himself."

She half smiled. Natalie loved special attention. "He's sweet."

"Celeste swears we're going to like the Sterns."

"She's a servant who's been dead for like two hundred years, she'd like anyone who didn't fire her." Natalie took a bite of her sandwich. "And the Sterns probably would if they could."

"Are they really that bad?"

She put down her sandwich. "It's just . . . I'm not used to having real parents around. I don't know how to act in front of them; I'm not good at pretending to be some normal kid who normal parents would like."

"Well, they're ghostkeepers, they can't really expect normal. Maybe they're okay."

"They haven't seen Bennett in forever, and the first thing they did was kick him out."

I popped a truffle in my mouth. "Yeah."

"Speaking of parents, how do you think Lukas is doing?"

"I don't know. I texted him this afternoon, but he didn't answer." Which worried me. "What if he doesn't come back?"

"Oh, he'll come back," Natalie said, her eyes narrowing. And I knew he would return, because she'd make it happen.

There was a knock at the door, and for moment I thought it must be Lukas, but then a woman's voice sounded. "Girls? Are you coming down for dinner?"

It was Mrs. Stern. Natalie and I stared at each other like we'd been caught in some nefarious scheme.

"No, thanks," I called through the door. "We've already eaten."

It took her a moment to respond, and I imagined her hand on the doorknob, wondering if she should confront us. Then she said, "All right. But we'll expect you tomorrow evening."

After she left, Natalie and I ranted about her. Who did she think she was? We'd go down to dinner if we damn well wanted to go down to dinner. But as we polished off our sandwiches, I think we were both pretty worried about our future at the Stern Museum.

That night, I stood at my bedroom window, hoping I'd see Bennett's Land Rover pull into the drive, knowing I wouldn't.

Instead, I saw a figure strolling through the maples. Coby! He hadn't been visiting much lately; he'd been spending his time with Harry and Sara, now that they knew he was a ghost. They couldn't see or hear him, but the three of them found ways to communicate.

I opened my window, a smile on my face—then realized it wasn't him. It was another ghost, a woman in a long white nightgown. I didn't recognize her in the distance, but for some reason she reminded me of mad Ophelia in Shakespeare's *Hamlet*. Like when she got closer, I'd see flowers woven through her hair and a crazy look in her eyes.

Except as she shifted from the darkness of the maples into the moonlight, I realized who she was. "Rachel?" I gasped.

I thought I saw her smile faintly before she turned, her attention suddenly on the distant tower of Thatcher, peeking over the museum's walls.

Aunt Rachel, I said, sputtering in surprise. *What . . . what are you—how are you—*

She didn't answer. She drifted in the direction of Thatcher, then faded into the Beyond before she hit the old stone wall.

Rachel was dead. I'd seen her die. No, I'd done more than that: I'd killed the wraith inside of her, the only thing keeping her alive.

And she was a ghostkeeper. Ghostkeepers didn't become ghosts unless they killed themselves, like Neos had, and then they went insane. Seeing Rachel was impossible.

I ransacked the room until I found my phone and dialed Bennett. He was the only other person still alive who was there for her death.

"I just saw Rachel's ghost," I blurted, as soon as he answered. "Out the window, she was here in the drive. She smiled at me and then went over the gates toward Thatcher."

"What? You can't have. It must've been someone else."

"Bennett, I think I'd know my own aunt."

"Really? Because you've only seen her once in ten years and she was possessed by a wraith."

Something about his tone set my back up. "I know what I saw."

"Emma, it doesn't make any sense."

"Maybe she didn't die."

He didn't respond, but I could hear him breathing into the phone, not wanting to argue with me, but not agreeing with me, either.

"Okay," I said, pacing the room. "She's dead. Then why did I see her ghost?"

"Because it wasn't Rachel. It has to be some other ghost."

He was right, of course. "What if it's a new kind of ghost that can shape-shift? Do you think Neos sent it here, looking like Rachel, to mess with me?"

"I've never heard of shape-shifting ghosts," he said.

"You'd never seen a wraith or a siren before you met me, either."

"That's true." He half laughed. "You really bring the fun, don't you?"

"Ouch," I said. That had been a direct hit.

"You know I didn't mean it like that."

"It's okay." I sighed into the phone. "I miss you."

"I know," he answered. But he didn't say it back, or tell me he loved me, or that he wished he were here kissing me.

"You're not going to get all cold and weird on me again, are you?" I didn't think I could handle that.

"No, it's just a mess here, after all the . . . trouble. The survivors are still grieving, and in shock. They put Simon in charge, but they hate that he isn't Yoshiro. It's not his fault, but he isn't exactly commanding."

"Give him a chance, Bennett. He's smart and he cares."

"I know," he said, with no conviction.

"You'll tell him about what I saw, right?"

"I'll tell him, but . . . there are a zillion more pressing things right now."

"Fine," I said. "I'll deal with it myself. I always do."

"Emma—be careful. I wish I were there, instead of here. The only person I want to be protecting is you." His voice changed. "Preferably under the covers with my lips pressed against yours."

I shivered at that last part. "That sounds good," I said softly into the phone. I lay down on the bed, imagining him beside me.

He started to say more when voices sounded in the background, calling his name, asking him something. "Em, I've got to go. If I were there, I'd kiss you good-bye. I guess I'll just have to say I love you."

"I love you."

After we hung up, I stared at the little clock on my iPhone: 10:58 p.m. Bennett had only been gone seven hours, but it felt like days—being separated from him was worse than ever.

3

After seeing Rachel's ghost—or whatever it was—and talking to Bennett, I barely slept. The next morning I stumbled downstairs into the kitchen, forgetting that the Sterns were in residence. Mr. Stern sat in the breakfast nook, looking fully rested, dressed, and composed, and eyed me with disfavor.

I'd tossed my gray silk robe over my red flannel pj's, only expecting to greet Anatole, waiting with a cup of tea. I'd grown used to his mustache twitching at the disheveled sight of me. Mr. Stern was another story.

I froze at the kitchen counter like a deer in headlights, hoping Natalie would suddenly appear to act as a buffer, but she was nowhere. Anatole and Celeste were on their best servant behavior and were lingering in the background.

"Good morning," Mr. Stern said, though his tone said "bad morning."

"Uh, I'm sorry." I adjusted my robe. "I didn't expect to see anyone." I tried for levity. "Well, except the ghosts."

"Which he can't see," Mrs. Stern said, entering the room from behind me. She smelled of expensive perfume and was dressed in a classic cream cashmere turtleneck over charcoal gray pants. Her expression was just as dour as his.

Crap. Of course; they were both ghostkeepers. He must've lost his powers to Mrs. Stern, and I'd just rubbed his face in it. Way to make another good impression. "I'm sorry. I should've—"

"You're sorry for a lot, aren't you?" Mr. Stern said. His clear blue eyes, so much like Bennett's, bored into me.

"Yeah, I—" I what? I didn't know what to tell them. How to say I was sorry about Olivia's death. That I didn't want Bennett to be taking Asarum any more than they did.

They were supposed to be my guardians, but they didn't exactly make it easy for me to ask for help. And I needed it. I didn't know what to do about the ghost I'd seen last night or how to find Neos. I longed for Simon, who was always such a great sounding board, but now was too busy with the Knell. I was back to feeling alone and unsure of myself, like when I'd first come to Echo Point.

"I'd better go," I said, and fled the room. They didn't try to stop me.

No matter how much I worried about it, or willed her to reappear, I didn't see Rachel's ghost again. Maybe I should've been relieved, but I couldn't shake a sense of dread. She'd disappeared in the direction of Thatcher, and by the time

Christmas Eve day rolled around, I realized if I was going to deal with this, I needed to check out the school. It was my only hope.

Natalie and I had gone into the village and bought a last-minute amaryllis plant for Mrs. Stern and "hermits" for Mr. Stern, which were a kind of raisin cookie. Natalie swore she'd heard him mention he had a "fondness" for them. We sort of hoped gifts would make them like us better, but it was doubtful. Then while Natalie knotted Christmas bows around the flower pot and cookie box, I flopped onto her bed and called Harry.

"Vaile," he answered. "Calling to wish me *felix dies Nativitatis*?"

"Oh. Sure. Merry Christmas."

He laughed. "Your enthusiasm overwhelms."

"How big's your tree?" I asked, wondering if they grew Christmas trees large enough to fill the great room in Harry's mansion.

"My tree is redwood big. You should come over and feel the spirit."

"We are talking about your Christmas tree, right?" Leave it to Harry to take it in some deviant direction.

"Oh. That tree. Also redwood big."

"*Anyway*," I said, "I called because I want to know if there's a way to sneak into Thatcher. The gates are locked." I'd walked up yesterday, just to take a look, and hadn't been able to get in.

"What makes you think I'd know?"

"Coby told me about the pig in the fireplace."

"You should've been there for that." He chuckled. "It was folkloric."

"Folkloric?"

"Like 'epic,' but on a smaller scale," he explained. "All right. Walk around campus, by the lower field. The back door of the field house is easy to pop open. You cut through the boys' lockers—avert your eyes, young Emma—and out the front door. Then to get into the main hall—"

"No," I stopped him. "That's enough. Thanks, Harry."

"What're you planning? Secret ghostly things?"

"Yeah."

"Well, if you decide to deck the halls with gay apparel, promise you'll invite me along."

I smiled. "You'll be the first I call."

"Namaste," he said, which he'd been saying since he got out of rehab. It wasn't growing on me.

Natalie glanced up from her bow. "Did he say 'namaste'? Tell him to namaste my ass."

"Natalie says—"

"I heard," he said. "Tell *her* anytime."

I snorted and hung up. "He said—"

She held up her hand. "I don't want to know. What I *do* want to know is, what are we doing at Thatcher?"

I liked that "we," but I said, "You don't have to go with me."

"Does it involve wraiths?"

"Doubtful."

"Ghasts?"

"Not that I know of."

Natalie stared at me. "Then what is it, Em? I can tell you're worked up about something."

I lay back on her bed. "Probably nothing," I said to the ceiling.

"But . . ."

"I think I saw Rachel's ghost three nights ago."

"Rachel, your aunt? I thought she was . . ."

"Yeah." I explained the whole story. I hadn't told her before because I thought she needed a break: time to get over Simon and Bennett being gone without worrying about a new threat. I wasn't sure what Rachel's ghost meant, but I couldn't help feeling Neos had sent her. I needed Natalie's help. There was no one else. "Bennett says I should find out more before bothering Simon about it."

"And you think she's at Thatcher?" Natalie asked.

"That's the direction she was heading."

Natalie glanced out the window. "Let's go before it gets dark."

"Good idea," I said, popping up.

"And bring your dagger," Natalie said.

"Deal."

We popped the door at the field house, just like Harry said, and I wished we really were there to play a prank. I was getting sick of chasing ghosts and fighting wraiths—battling Neos will do that to you. And Natalie was acting nervous, which worried me. She was the gutsy one, rushing headlong into danger, knowing I'd clean up the mess. But today, she held back.

Without anyone around, Thatcher felt weird, sort of sad. A heavy silence was broken only by the hollow rush of the wind. The day was bitter cold, and I couldn't tell if I was imagining an edge of malevolence in the air.

"I don't like this," Natalie said. "This is the kind of thing that turns out nasty for us."

"I know. Anytime we go looking for ghosts, wraiths or ghasts jump out at us. Maybe I imagined Rachel. It was late, and I was upset about Bennett leaving. Let's just do a little summoning and get out of here."

She gave a short unhappy nod, and we wandered through the grounds together, but not too close. I think we both would've preferred to hold hands, but we'd tried that before and discovered our powers were completely different. We worked better apart.

But not today. Today neither of us could summon Rachel. Neither of us could summon anything other than the usual Thatcher ghosts. The campus used to belong to my ancestor Emma, who'd lived here over two hundred years ago, and I felt a connection to it, yet I couldn't detect any trace of Rachel. It was almost as though my ability was being blocked. I felt as though something was threatening us—I just couldn't figure out what it could be. If it were a ghost, I should be able to summon it.

I tried to shake off the sense of foreboding as we circled the grounds in the chilly late afternoon, not talking much, instead opening ourselves to the spectral traces of the Beyond as we probed with our summoning powers. We split up when we hit the running track that encircled the football field.

I went along the bleachers, across the end zone, and stopped at the equipment shack, where I caught a whiff of something, but when I focused my power, it was gone. The field was covered in a white blanket of dull snow in the failing sunlight, and wisps of moisture rose here and there, which struck me as strange. How was there moisture in the air, when the temperature was below freezing?

As the wisps uncoiled, they started thickening, turning from thin threads of moisture to heavy ropes. They swayed and rose, like snakes from a basket, and the stench suddenly struck me: ashes. Hot ashes and burning smoke, which stung my eyes even though the wind was cold.

My throat clenched in fear, and I searched the shadows for Natalie. She was across the field, looking completely oblivious to the smoky serpents uncoiling from the snow.

"Nat—" I started to call.

I trailed off when the smoke twisted into what looked like a gaunt man, composed of a dozen writhing snakes, near the 50-yard line. He didn't look like Neos, but I understood that's who he represented, and I summoned my dispelling power to ward him off. Yet I felt no ghosts in the area. It was almost like having a flashback, yet there hadn't been that familiar whirling sensation. This was a vision I couldn't control.

I watched, helplessly, as this terrifying, smoky version of Neos raised one serpentine arm, gesturing to another cluster of snakes writhing in a mound next to him—a feeding frenzy of snapping fangs and lashing tails. There was something *underneath* the mound: a person. And with a sudden rush of knowledge that left me breathless, I realized that person was me.

Being eaten alive by snakes.

Goose bumps rose on my arms, and I called my power closer and stronger—but still couldn't find any ghostly presence. Then the wisps of smoke formed a third figure across the field, and my heart almost unclenched. Bennett. Come to rescue me.

Except he didn't help the girl trapped in the writhing pile. Instead, he strode across the field, sucking the life from the snakes, growing stronger and stronger. And when he finally approached the girl, he prepared to suck the life out of *her*, too. I felt frozen, unable to stop what was happening.

"No!" I screamed—and the scene disappeared.

No serpents, no smoky Neos. No Bennett, no me. Not a tinge of ghostly power in the air. Just the snowy field, and the almost-overpowering scent of ashes.

Natalie came running, her summoning energy crackling around her. "What's wrong?"

"I—I saw something." I breathed to slow my heartbeat. "It's gone now."

"What was it?"

"S-smoke," I stuttered. "Snakes made of smoke. Can you smell that?"

She sniffed. "I don't smell anything."

The stench of ashes still thickened the air and clung to my hair and coat. "I think I had a vision. Do you feel any ghosts nearby?"

She shook her head. "Not even a little."

"Me, neither." I swallowed and looked at the now-normal field. "Nothing."

"Are you okay?" she asked, eyeing me with concern.

"Yeah, it was just . . . scary." I looked at the darkening sky. "Let's go."

"Best idea of the day." Natalie hooked her arm through mine and steered me quickly back through the field house as I told her about the vision—everything except Bennett. Everyone already suspected he was losing his mind on Asarum; I couldn't make them think even worse of him.

"It's not the first time," I said, as we crunched down the gravel drive of the museum. "I dreamed of them before. Back in San Francisco. A vision or something, of them coming from my dad's funeral urns. It totally freaked me out, and I almost told you about it, but I thought you were someone else back then."

"Don't take this the wrong way," she said, "but is it possible you're imagining all of it? I didn't sense anything back there. And neither did you. If it was ghosts, we should've been able to feel it. You're tired, Em. And now Simon and Lukas and Bennett are all gone, and we're left with his crummy parents. It wouldn't be too surprising if you were just kind of . . . losing it."

"Yeah," I said, again feeling confused and unsure of myself. "Maybe I'm just tired." I suddenly wanted my mom. Or Martha. Someone to feed me soup and tell me everything would be all right.

Then we opened the front door and found Mrs. Stern staring at us. She was dressed in a cream silk blouse, black velvet pants, and pearls, and I couldn't tell if she'd overheard us talking.

"I wondered when you'd get back," she said. "Dinner's in half an hour. You might . . ." She glanced at our jeans and boots. "You might want to change, but it's up to you."

And suddenly I remembered it was Christmas Eve. And my parents hadn't come. And I was back to having mysterious visions that nobody else could see.

I scrubbed my face, willing away the memory of the smoky snakes. Afraid of what it meant. Not wanting to believe what it said about Bennett, or that Neos was somehow controlling my visions—I couldn't think of any other explanation. Except maybe Natalie was right, and I was just exhausted.

It was Christmas Eve. I should've been focusing on that. Except I didn't want to spend Christmas without my parents. Why couldn't they have come? How could they not understand that sometimes I needed them?

Feeling depressed, I went for the long, soft black sweater in my wardrobe, leggings, and black flats instead of my boots, a clear sign I was dressing up. I swished some toothpaste in my mouth, ran styling stick through my hair, and applied lip gloss.

I found Natalie in the hallway and stopped short. She was wearing khaki pants, a white shirt buttoned to the neck, and a boxy royal blue crewneck sweater. Conservative and shapeless, she looked nothing like herself.

"Are those *slacks*?" I asked.

She frowned. "I just want to look normal."

"Natalie, dressing like Mr. Rogers isn't going to make Bennett's parents like you."

Her shoulders slumped. "Whatever."

"You look cute," I said, trying again. "Kind of, um, retro-ironic?"

"Let's go," she muttered, like we were off to the guillotine.

We'd eaten dinner with Mr. and Mrs. Stern—they hadn't asked us to call them John and Alexandra—for the past three nights. Things hadn't gotten better since my confrontation with them that morning in the kitchen. The first night, my one conversational gambit had been to ask them where they'd been living in Europe.

"Paris," Mr. Stern had answered in his low voice.

"Have you been?" Mrs. Stern asked.

I had, but I was so young I didn't remember it. Natalie and I both shook our heads, and that had ended that conversation.

Even their sporadic chitchat made me nervous, like their words concealed hidden meanings and unvoiced accusations that I was to blame for their daughter's death and Bennett's addiction. Natalie didn't fare much better. If she acted like herself, bright and loud and a little outrageous, they looked puzzled and dismayed. I guess that's why she'd dressed like someone else entirely tonight.

We wandered into the formal dining room. The long mahogany table was set beautifully, with a china pattern I hadn't yet seen. Wreaths of holly surrounded a silver candelabra filled with pale candles already lit. I noticed the thread of smoke rising from a candle and almost panicked, thinking it would take the shape of a snake. I took a few deep breaths. No ashes, no snakes. Just smoke. And the room was perfumed with the scent of beeswax combined with the boughs of pine hanging from the fireplace. So far, the best thing about spending Christmas in New England was the decorations. The real fir trees and pinecones and fresh wreaths that always looked a little out of place in San Francisco fit perfectly in Echo Point's old houses.

The Sterns weren't there, but Celeste was flitting around the table making last-minute adjustments.

You've outdone yourself, I told her. *Sorry Natalie and I weren't here to help.*

Celeste curtsied. *Merci. But that iz not your place. And thingz are not as zey were. Iz better I do alone.*

I was about to ask why when Mrs. Stern came strolling in and surveyed the table. "This looks lovely, Celeste."

And with a wave of her hand, she compelled Celeste toward the kitchen. Huh. I knew she was a ghostkeeper, but I hadn't thought much about her powers. Turns out she was a pretty powerful compeller—not to mention pretty rude, ordering Celeste around like a dog.

"Natalie," Mrs. Stern said. "Why don't you sit here, and Emma on the other side. John had some business, but will be here soon."

"You're going to let her get away with that?" Natalie whispered.

I shrugged as I took my seat. I didn't really want to give Bennett's mom one more reason to dislike me. On the other hand . . . it really bugged me.

"Celeste is dead, Mrs. Stern," I said, putting my napkin in my lap. "She's not deaf."

"Pardon me?"

"You don't need to compel her to do things. You can just *ask*."

"I'm sure Celeste doesn't mind, Emma," she said, a little flustered.

"Celeste wouldn't mind if you used her as a footstool. That doesn't make it okay."

She gazed at me for a long moment, and I wished I'd kept my mouth shut. She was that scary. But Mr. Stern stepped into the room before she could respond. He was wearing a navy button-down tucked into khaki pants and a frown, and he looked almost surprised to see us there.

"Girls," he said briefly, before settling at the head of the table.

Natalie and I eyed Mrs. Stern warily, but she apparently decided to let my little outburst go.

And thus began the Christmas Eve from hell. Oh, it

was beautiful and elegant, and Anatole had seriously outdone himself with the food, as though he'd only been waiting for the Sterns to return home to show us what he was made of. But we ate each course in silence, our silver tinkling on the china.

Christmas Eve with strangers. The Sterns were no doubt mourning their first Christmas without Olivia and Bennett, while Natalie had to live with the fact that her parents didn't love and accept her. And I was left trying to ignore that vision and wondering where my own family was. Investigating Neos, no doubt, but at least they could've called.

At the end of the meal, Natalie and I stood to help Celeste clear the plates, but Mrs. Stern waved a hand and said, "That won't be necessary."

Somehow, that long uncomfortable meal had sapped all my strength, so I didn't say anything. Instead, we both sunk into our chairs for another stony ten minutes, while Celeste bustled around us.

"What's up with this? It's like you're miming a Christmas dinner," a male voice said.

"Lukas!" Natalie jumped up at the sight of him in his black down jacket, jeans, and Timberlands, striding into the dining room with a grin on his face. "You're back."

"And none too soon." He took in her outfit. "Did you turn Amish while I was gone?"

"No, I'm not Amish, you idiot," she said, but she didn't sound mad about it and hugged him.

He reluctantly let Natalie go and turned to the Sterns.

"I'm sorry—I feel like I'm interrupting a moment of silence or something."

"You must be Lukas," Mrs. Stern said stiffly. "We're Alexandra and John Stern."

"Bennett's parents." Lukas glanced at me. "*Excellent.*"

"Yup," I said flatly, but the look I gave Lukas made it clear how much I thought this development sucked.

"Right," Lukas said, shaking Mr. Stern's hand. "Pleased to meet you. So where's Bennett?"

"Away," Mr. Stern answered shortly.

"What are you doing here?" Natalie asked Lukas. "What happened with your mom and dad?"

Lukas shook his head. "Nothing good. It was like a twenty-car pileup."

"I understand your parents aren't ghostkeepers," Mrs. Stern said.

"They're the opposite of ghostkeepers." Lukas tossed his jacket on a side chair. "They're ghosthaters. At least, I guess they believe me now. They just want me to stop doing it."

Mr. Stern put his arm around Lukas's shoulder. "Well, you're welcome here. Come sit down."

Natalie and I exchanged glances. Why were they suddenly being so nice?

"It can be so tough when it doesn't run in the family," Mrs. Stern said sympathetically. "I'm sorry to hear it didn't go well—but at least you're here now, among friends. Are you hungry?"

"Starved," Lukas said, and a moment later Celeste

came in carrying a tray bearing a full meal for him. Mrs. Stern must've compelled it from all the way in the kitchen. A nice trick, but I wondered if she only did it to show me she'd compel Celeste anytime she wanted.

"Thanks, C," Lukas told Celeste, which almost made me smile. At least *he* was no longer compelling her around.

He sat beside Natalie and dug in. "Oh man, this is so good."

"Anatole is a treasure," Mr. Stern agreed.

"Is that not the best soup you ever tasted?" Mrs. Stern asked, a slight grin on her face. It was so sudden and charming, coming from her. "I told Anatole he should sell the recipe, and you should've seen his face. He was scandalized."

Lukas laughed and slurped another spoonful, while the Sterns chatted away, clearly trying to make him comfortable. Natalie and I gaped at each other. What had brought on this change? Did they only hate girls?

"Where's Simon?" Lukas asked, around a bite of soufflé.

"They've made him head of the Knell," I answered.

Lukas set his fork down. "Bennett's gone, his parents are back, and Simon's the head of the Knell? I was only gone for four days."

"Too long," Natalie murmured.

Lukas paused a moment before going back to his meal. "I don't suppose there's seconds?"

"There's dessert," Mrs. Stern said, nodding toward Celeste carrying a cake on a silver platter.

"Christmas cake," Mr. Stern explained as Celeste laid a

plate before each of us. It was a brownish cake with nuts and raisins and hard white frosting. "We were stationed in England for many years when the children were younger."

"Stationed by the Knell?" I asked. "They actually post people places?"

"We volunteered," Mrs. Stern answered. "They were having a run on ghasts. John no longer has his powers, but he's a wonderful tactician, and the children and I make—*made*—a good team."

This was news to me. Bennett had fought ghasts with his mom and sister? Maybe that partly explained his devotion to them. You couldn't get closer than battling evil ghosts together.

Mrs. Stern got a far-off look in her eyes, and for a moment I wondered if she was going to cry. Then she folded her napkin tightly, as though she could control her emotions just as neatly.

I stared at my plate; maybe I should cut them some slack. Mr. Stern had lost his powers for love—and he and Mrs. Stern both lost their daughter to Neos. They were cold and difficult, but they were also hurting.

"Anyway." Mr. Stern cleared his throat, possibly not wanting to dwell on the past. "They make this cake. You bake it in October and don't eat it until now."

"Like a Twinkie experiment," Lukas said, prodding his cake with his fork. "Except this is definitely decaying."

"Dare you," I said to him.

"Maybe they shouldn't have it," Mrs. Stern said blandly. "There's an awful lot of alcohol. They could get a little tipsy."

That was all we needed to hear. The three of us each took an enormous bite.

"It's weird," Natalie said, making a face.

Lukas gazed into the fire. "Tastes like . . . I don't know, like nothing I've ever tasted."

"Peat moss," I suggested. "It tastes like peat moss."

"I told you they wouldn't like it." Mr. Stern gave Mrs. Stern a morose look, and I felt bad I'd made fun of his cake.

Lukas swallowed his second bite. "But *delicious* peat moss."

"And the frosting's perfect," I said, licking it off my fork.

Mr. Stern made a *hmph*ing sound, but I could tell he was pleased.

"John's mad he doesn't get to eat it all himself," Mrs. Stern told Lukas. "He likes to sneak into the pantry and cut off chunks well into January."

We finished our meal, and I stood in the doorway, ready to escape upstairs. We'd survived Christmas Eve. But as I looked at the Sterns, I couldn't help but feel a little sorry for them.

"I know you probably didn't want us here," I blurted. "Three teenagers who can't make things work with their own parents. Nobody wants that. So, thank you. For letting us stay here and for sharing your holiday with us."

"And your dessert," Lukas added.

"Yeah," Natalie said. "Thanks."

"Oh," Mr. Stern said, looking startled. "Of course."

And I wondered if things were going to get better, now that Lukas was back. The ice was officially broken.

Then I noticed Mrs. Stern. She had a funny look on her face I couldn't decipher, but I was pretty certain it wasn't positive.

As we headed upstairs, Lukas said to Natalie, "Dude, you say you're not Amish, but what are you wearing?"

"Shut up," she said, but there was no venom in her voice, only happiness.

Okay, so maybe the ice was only cracked, but I was still glad Lukas was back. And he made Natalie happy, too.

4

That night I dreamed of a man made of smoky snakes. The snakes untwined from his body and slithered around me, wrapping me tight, squeezing the life from me. Just as they were covering my face and mouth, I woke. My heart raced and I couldn't catch my breath. The sky outside my window was a crisp blue, and the scent of something sweet wafted from downstairs—but inside I knew something was wrong.

I reached under the extra pillow on my bed for my dagger.

"You sleep with a knife under your pillow? I had no idea." Bennett sprawled in the chair beside the dresser. He looked tense, but amused. "Did you have a nightmare?"

"How long have you been there? You scared me." I started to calm down. "And I sleep with it in case I wake up and find a strange man in my bedroom." I stuffed the dagger back under the pillow.

He held a paper cup with a plastic lid—it was the chai

I'd smelled—and he'd started a blaze in the little fireplace. I'd missed having a fire since Nicholas was gone. But all I really cared about was that Bennett was back. It'd been four cold, lonely days without him. And that dream had left me feeling shaky.

There was a glint in his eyes. "I've seen you use it; I'm glad I'm not strange."

"That's debatable," I quipped, just feeling so grateful to see him. I was glad it hadn't been him in my dream. I wanted to believe that he'd always be my safety net. "What are you doing here?"

"Will that ever get old? When this is over and we're finally together forever, I'm going to have to invent new ways to surprise you, just so you can say that to me."

Together forever. I liked the sound of that. I liked when he was the surprise, too.

He handed me the chai and sat beside me on the bed. I took a comforting sip, trying not to recall what happened last time he'd brought me one. But I did remember—he'd disappeared for a month. I didn't know why everyone I loved went missing. I think they all thought I was stronger than I really was. At least Bennett came back.

I pulled the covers higher, suddenly self-conscious about my unsexy red flannel pajamas.

"I'm sorry," he said, "for being such an ass on the phone the other night. The Knell's in rough shape. As a kid I always thought they were like James Bond meets Jason Bourne—unstoppable. But now . . ." He shrugged. "I took it out on you, and that's not fair."

I put my chai on the bedside table. "That's okay. I can't expect you to drop everything for me whenever I call. Although . . ."

"What?"

"You could drop everything and kiss me."

And he did. Until I finally pulled back, breathless and dizzy, and inspected his face. I didn't want to admit it, but he looked even worse than when he'd left four days ago.

"I know," he said. "I look bad. You don't have to say it, Em. It's changing me. Not just how I look, but my mood, the way I think . . ."

"So, are you going to stop?" I asked in a small voice.

"Not yet." For a moment, neither of us spoke. He leaned his head back against the wall. "Merry Christmas, right?" He grimaced. "Doesn't feel that merry this year, does it?"

"No," I agreed. "Natalie and I are on a complete anti-Christmas kick."

"Still. I got you something." He held out one of those little silk Chinese purses, magenta with white embroidery, just big enough to hold a piece of jewelry. I loved the iPhone he'd given me at Thanksgiving, but I couldn't help agreeing with Celeste, a little jewelry was nice.

I unsnapped the lid and pulled out a ring, a hammered silver band like the one he wore on his own finger.

"I know," he said, running a hand through his dark hair in a gesture I recognized as embarrassment. "Matching rings? Lame. But I passed the place where I bought mine, and I was thinking of you, so . . ." He shrugged. "You don't have to wear it."

"I love it." I slipped it on the ring finger of my right hand. "It's not lame at all."

I hopped out of bed and opened my top dresser drawer. Inside was a package wrapped in red paper with a green ribbon. "I got you something, too."

His eyes lit up, and I tried not to notice how they were tinged with red, his irises lacking their usual brilliance. I handed the box to him and he ripped it open. Inside was a silver pocketknife I'd found at one of the antique shops in the village.

"I thought I shouldn't be the only one to have a knife around here."

He looked pleased as he ran his fingers over the design engraved in the side. "Cool. I never had a pocketknife."

"Really? And here I thought you had everything," I teased.

There was an intent, knowing look on his face as he gently pulled me toward him. "The only thing I want is you."

We fell onto the bed together and started to undo each other's clothing. Let me just say, red plaid flannel pajamas suddenly become very sexy when your bad-boy boyfriend is unbuttoning them while kissing his way down your neck. With the first kiss, I could feel my tension ease. I let everything go as his hands slid down my body. My sighs only encouraged him.

"Oh God, Emma," he whispered into my ear, causing me to shiver. "You don't know what you do to me."

Then, like an echo: "Oh God. Emma!" but more

forcefully, and with my mother's voice. I pushed away from Bennett and saw her in the doorway. "Mom!" And then, "Dad!"

My father hovered behind my mom, a horrified expression on his face. Poor guy. The idea of me being with a boy was repugnant to him. I'd probably just given him a year's worth of nightmares. But seriously, they had to show up now? They couldn't have called first and told me not to worry, they'd be here Christmas morning? I was miserable last night without them.

No. Instead they show up without warning and interrupt what had been turning into the highlight of my winter vacation.

"Does the word *knock* mean nothing to you?" I snapped. "This is ridiculous. *Again*?"

I felt Bennett stifle a laugh. "Could we be any more doomed?" he muttered.

"Emma, button your top," my mother said.

"Do you really think you can waltz in here after leaving me on my own for months and months, and start bossing—"

"Please, Emma," my mother implored. "For your father."

I grumbled, but took pity on my dad and buttoned my top. Bennett looked amused. Guys think it's funny when they've been caught in flagrante*—for a dead language, Latin could sometimes be quite apt—but, as a girl, I was supposed to feel ashamed.

---

* While blazing

Well, I wasn't ashamed. Okay, I was a little embarrassed, but mostly I was pissed. At everyone in my life for appearing and disappearing whenever they felt like it. At having this power I didn't ask for, and all the responsibilities that went with it. I could feel my skin begin to prickle with pent-up anger and frustration.

"Get out!" I said. "All of you."

"Emma— " my father started.

"Please! Can I just get dressed in peace?" I was close to breaking down, and my voice cracked. "Is that too much to ask?"

Bennett rested his hand on my shoulder for a second, then stood. He sort of herded my parents into the hallway, then shot me one last look before closing the door behind him.

I flopped back on the bed and screamed into my pillow.

I took a long shower and stressed about my parents. Had they only come back for the holiday, or were they here to take me home to San Francisco? I couldn't leave without finishing Neos—they had to know that, right? As I dried off and dressed, I tried to figure out how I'd convince them to let me stay. Then I worried that maybe the Sterns had called them to take me away.

I didn't want to be thinking about any of that. I fingered the heavy silver band Bennett had given me. It was Christmas, and all I wanted to do was focus on my boyfriend surprising me with his presence and his present—so I spent some time making myself presentable. No stains on my gray sweater or black skirt, and no runs in my black patterned tights. I added some blush to my lip-gloss-and-styling-stick routine, but wiped it off because it made me look like I had a sunburn. Still, I looked better than I usually did. Though I think Bennett would've preferred me *out* of my clothes.

When I stepped into the hallway, I found Lukas leaning against the wall outside my door, looking repentant.

"What's up with you?"

"Dude, I'm sorry," he said. "Your parents asked me where your room was."

I gaped at him. "And you told them?"

"I had no idea Bennett was in there with you," he explained.

Natalie's door swung open. "Your parents came?" Her expression was a little forlorn, or maybe jealous, I couldn't tell. Then her face changed, like a light switching on. "So wait, not only did *Bennett's* parents find you guys together, but now *yours* did, too?"

"Yup."

"No!" She started giggling. "Oh, God! Were you naked again?"

"When was she naked?" Lukas asked.

Natalie gasped out an explanation between giggles. Halfway through, Lukas started laughing, too.

"I wasn't naked! At least, not all the way." Which for

some reason they found even funnier. "We are so cursed," I mumbled, and marched downstairs into the fray.

I found them all in the kitchen. My parents sat huddled in the breakfast nook across from Bennett and his parents, all of them looking awkward and unhappy.

"There you are," my mother said.

"Yeah," I said. "*I'm* the one who's hard to track down."

My father murmured something like, "Now, now, Emma," then everyone fell silent.

Celeste handed me a cup of tea, steeped for a long time with a splash of milk, just the way I liked it. There was no room for me at the table, so Bennett got up and I slid into his place as he leaned against the kitchen counter. Nobody said anything. I took a bite of the cinnamon bun Bennett had abandoned and glanced at Anatole hovering near the stove. *These are perfect*, I told him. *Like always*. Then I added, *Can you believe how awkward this is? Are the French this ridiculous?*

Worze, Celeste said.

Impossible, I told her. I took another contemplative bite. *They are missing one thing*.

Anatole's mustache bristled. *You are suggesting I forget zomething? Thiz iz reediculuz! What iz your so-called missing ingredient?*

Arsenic.

He snorted a laugh, and Celeste *tsk*ed at me from near the sink, though I'm pretty sure I saw her smiling.

"If you're talking to *them*," my father said, "you can talk to *us*."

"Emma doesn't owe you anything." Bennett set his coffee cup down hard on the counter. "You left her to fend for herself in San Francisco."

"And you took full advantage of that," my mom said.

"At least *I* got her somewhere safe. You left her alone, and never even told her who she was. You tried to have her powers destroyed."

I was glad Bennett was here, voicing my position. Somehow I'd never been able to say these things to them myself. He made me feel like I had a right to be angry.

"We *tried* to protect her," my dad said. "You have no idea what she attracted just walking down the street. Then Neos found her." He took a deep breath. "We didn't know what to do."

"You should've gone to the Knell," Bennett's father said in his deep voice. "They could've protected her."

"No, Dad, we couldn't," Bennett scoffed. "We couldn't even protect ourselves."

Right again. I wanted to jump in, but he was on a roll. And honestly, I was worried I'd say things I couldn't take back.

"If they'd gone to the Knell," his mother said, her voice tight, "Neos wouldn't have searched San Francisco. He wouldn't have found Olivia. He wouldn't have—" She swallowed.

She held her head high and didn't quite look at me,

and I knew she wished it was me who was dead, instead of her daughter.

"I can't imagine how difficult that is," my mother told her, surprisingly gently. "And I—"

"Don't you dare," Bennett snarled at his mother. "Don't you even *think* about putting Olivia's death on Emma."

This is where we finally differed. I knew Neos was ultimately responsible for Olivia's death, but I still wondered if things could've been different.

"I'm not," his mother snapped back. "I'm saying that if Jana and Nathan did the responsible thing—"

"Now, now," Bennett's father said, his voice placating. "There's no way to—"

"If *we* did the responsible thing?" my dad said, his face reddening. "Are you suggesting—"

"Olivia only moved to California to get away from *you*," Bennett said. "If she—"

Everyone started yelling at once. I could only catch snippets of what was said, and felt like my brain was going to explode.

"Don't you speak to your mother like—"

"—and almost got killed fighting Neos, while the Knell stood by and—"

"—walking around like a junkie—"

It was time to break my code of silence.

"Stop!" I screamed. "Just stop!" My voice echoed around the kitchen. When they quieted down, I continued. "Don't you see none of this matters? We have to find Neos, that's all. After we stop him, I don't care—you can lock yourselves in a room and argue for months."

My father rubbed his face with his palm. "You're right. She's right. But how are we going to stop him?"

"I don't know," I admitted. "The only thing I can think of is trying to find that ghost I saw. Maybe it wasn't Rachel, but I know it was connected to Neos."

"What?" my dad said. "You saw Rachel's ghost?"

"Or a shape-shifter, I guess."

Mr. Stern furrowed his brow. "That's not possible, is it? I've never heard of such a thing."

"When was this?" Mrs. Stern asked me. "Why didn't you tell us? You must tell us about any unusual event immediately."

"Alexandra is right," my mom said. "We have to know these things if we're going to help you, Emma. Tell us about this ghost."

All four parents gazed at me with impatient parental attention. Well, at least they'd found something to agree on. I drained my teacup and told them. But not about my vision in the field at Thatcher. Because I didn't want to know what it was trying to tell me about Bennett.

Late that afternoon, we sat down to Christmas dinner. I worried that Lukas and Natalie would feel left out, but my parents took an interest in Natalie, and for some reason, Lukas was still a hit with the Sterns.

The food was even more spectacular than last night, and the meal much more comfortable, like yelling at each other had released some of the pressure. Bennett's mom didn't correct me when I cleared the dishes with Celeste or when Natalie and Lukas helped her with the dessert plates. Bennett topped off all the parents' wineglasses and gave each of us underage units half a glass, then sat down next to me and scooted his chair closer, so our legs were pressed together. As he laid his arm across the back of my chair, his fingers lightly caressing my shoulder, I felt something I almost didn't recognize.

Happiness.

I was happy that my parents came, even if I wished my brother Max had come with them. I was happy that Bennett was here, even if he didn't look entirely himself. I was happy his parents were warming up, chatting and drinking, even smiling. I was happy Lukas and Natalie looked content—like they knew that they weren't guests at the table, they were family, too. I almost let myself forget everything that was ahead of me: school, finding Rachel's ghost, and killing Neos.

There was a billiard room in the museum, which sometimes made me feel like I was living in a game of Clue. Shortly after dinner, my dad headed off to play pool with Bennett, his dad, and Lukas. Having realized the futility of conservative clothing, Natalie sashayed in behind them, wearing a denim mini, tall boots, and a magenta sweater hanging off one shoulder. She was either going to cheerlead or show them all how it was done—it was always hard to guess with her.

I don't know where Bennett's mom disappeared to, but I found mine on the sofa in the front parlor, leafing through a design book she wasn't really reading. I loved the pale sea-green walls in the parlor and the simple antique furnishings, but Neos had killed Martha here. She'd been Bennett and Olivia's nanny, but to me, even though we'd only known each other a short time, she'd been more like the grandmother I'd never had. I hadn't spent any time in this room since her death.

I stood in the doorway and let the memories fade, then studied my mom. She looked less haggard than when she'd visited me at the hospital, but still skinnier than before she left San Francisco, and a little fidgety. When she noticed me, she set her book aside and smiled.

I almost started to tell her about Martha, but instead said, "Hi," as I entered the room. Everything had been so crazy, I hadn't had the chance to say that simple word.

Her smile widened. "I missed you. No one says 'hi' like you do."

"What's so special about it?"

"I don't know. It's just *you.*" She stood and hugged me.

The scent of her shampoo made me smile. "I missed you, too. Are you back for good this time?"

"Well . . . ," she said as we sat on the French-blue velvet sofa. "That's really up to you."

"What do you mean?" I asked. "And where's Max?"

"Neos isn't the only evil ghost on the planet. Max really was in Tibet, just not on exchange. He's been working with a small village to help them dispel a tenacious ghost. He'll be here soon." She pushed a lock of hair out of my face. "I want to hear about you."

I started talking. I told her about seeing the tapestry at the Knell with the image of a previous Emma who looked exactly like me. I told her about losing Martha—then losing Coby. About losing my old friend Abby, too, in a different way, and finding Natalie and Lukas, and Harry and Sara, who'd become more than friends to me. I told her about the fight at the Knell, about Nicholas and Rachel and all the leaders of the Knell who'd died. I told her about fighting wraiths and facing Neos: about beating him, too, except he never stayed beaten. He always came back, stronger than ever.

I spoke nonstop for an hour, not quite believing how much had happened over the last few months. Or how painful it was to relive all of it, except for the good friends I'd made.

My mother listened. She hugged me when I needed it, and she apologized when I needed that. And no, she'd never been the mom who baked cookies or went on school field trips, but maybe that wasn't the kind of mother I'd needed. Because she hadn't always been there for me, smoothing the way, I'd learned to make my own choices. I came from a long line of powerful ghostkeepers—I needed to trust my own strength.

"And what about Bennett?" she asked lightly, fiddling with her earring.

"I don't know," I answered truthfully. "I love him, and he loves me. I know that. But he's taking Asarum because he's determined to fight Neos with me; he doesn't want me to have to face that alone. But it's changing him. And what happens when Neos is finally gone? Ghostkeeping and the Knell are Bennett's life. No matter how much I want to be with him, I can't let him give that up."

She nodded briefly, as one of her legs jiggled to a twitchy beat. I forgot that's exactly what she'd done for my dad: given up her ghostkeeping powers.

"I've stopped, you know. Taking Asarum." She noticed me noticing her leg and forced herself to sit still. She hadn't stopped fidgeting since we'd sat down. "It hasn't been easy."

"You look better," I said, despite the tense energy.

She nodded. "I feel better. Would you like me to talk to Bennett?"

"Would you? Not just about the Asarum. But about . . ."

"Giving up my powers?"

"Yeah."

"I will." She smoothed her hair. "There is a slight problem, though."

I frowned. "What?"

"We want you to come with us," my father said from the doorway.

"Come where?" I asked.

"To the Knell."

"What? Why? I thought you hated them."

"Not 'hated'—mistrusted. They're complacent and rigid and—" He stopped. "Well, they *were*. It's a different story now. And Simon is brilliant, discovering the principle of reflexivity, and—"

"The what?"

"The principle of reflexivity," he repeated. "That ghost-keeping powers work both ways. Readers like me can also imprint messages. Compellers can release compulsion, communicators can silence ghosts, and summoners can banish them."

I nodded. "He taught us some of that. What about dispellers?" I asked, thinking of Bennett.

"They can heal," my father said. "At least, that's what Simon suspects."

"The *point* is," my mother said, amused by my father's enthusiasm, "Simon's asked us to help them rebuild. Emma, we want you to move with us to the city."

They wanted me with them. Wasn't that what I'd needed to hear all this time? I felt a flush of pleasure, but the second thoughts came at once. "Bennett's there," I said. "If he sees me every day, he'll *never* stop taking Asarum."

"He'll never stop anyway," my mother said. "He's addicted, Emma. I only took a fraction of what Bennett's doing, and I'm still struggling. Bennett's not going to kick it."

"Of course he will," I insisted. "Once Neos is gone. He can't go on like that forever."

She shook her head sadly. "Your being there won't be the deciding factor."

My father kissed the top of my head. "We've made a lot of mistakes, Emma. Come with us. Let us try to fix a few of them."

"I can't go," I said, though I didn't understand my own certainty. "That ghost I saw—even if it isn't Rachel, she's the key to finding Neos. I know it. I have to stay and find her." And figure out what that vision meant.

"Let the Sterns find her," Dad told me. "And Natalie and Lukas."

"Emma, please," Mom said. "You should be with us. You're only seventeen, and we—we miss you."

"I love you," I told them.

I saw relief etched in their faces, like they hadn't been sure. My mother stopped bouncing her foot long enough to hug me. "We love you, too."

"But I can't go with you," I said into my mom's shoulder.

She pulled back and searched my face. "Emma—"

"Nothing can happen to Natalie or Lukas. They're my . . ." I faltered, suddenly understanding the reason I needed to stay, but afraid I was going to start crying instead of explaining. "You don't know how dangerous Neos is. I'm the only one who can stop him. And Natalie and Lukas don't have anyone else. Their own parents suck—even worse than you—and I can't leave Sara with Coby dead and Harry just out of rehab. They need me. I can't let them down."

My mom gave my father a look across the top of my head, and I glanced at him for his reaction.

"What?" I asked. "Why are you smiling?"

"Because we don't suck as parents," my mom said.

I half grinned. "Well . . ."

"Look at you, Emma," Dad said, his eyes shining. "We did *something* right. We couldn't be more proud of you."

And then I did cry. Because even though I pretended to be all tough and independent, I loved hearing that from them.

"I can stay here?" I asked, through sniffles.

"You can stay."

5

Not the Christmas from hell after all, I realized, climbing into bed that night. Not bad, if you didn't count my parents walking in on me and Bennett, or the scene around the breakfast nook.

I reached to turn out the light, and heard a crinkling noise from the hallway. I grabbed my dagger—wondering yet again how I became the kind of girl who slept with a knife—and listened intently. Silence. I crept toward the door, and my toe nudged a piece of paper that had been shoved through the crack.

I smiled, expecting a love note from Bennett. But the handwriting looked shaky and weird, almost spidery. *Meet me in the solarium. Come alone.*

I probed the paper with my reading ability and sensed some ghostly resonance, but no menace. And no mental pictures, either, which was strange. Was it from the ghost that looked like Rachel?

I paused outside Natalie's door on my way downstairs,

wondering if I should wake her. Or Bennett. Or, hell, my parents were here—let them deal with one of these messes for once. But I was afraid that whoever sent the note would disappear if I didn't come alone, and I wanted to know who—or what—it was.

I could protect myself, and tried to comfort myself with that thought as I tiptoed down the grand staircase. But I could feel my heart racing as I crossed the kitchen into the solarium. I stood in the moonlight and silence, smelling the tang of the citrus trees, as I sent out tendrils of summoning power, trying to find a ghost, hoping I wouldn't have another vision of the snaky ghost man.

A deep voice from behind a lemon bush asked, "Have I told you how much I love those pajamas?"

"Bennett!" I dropped my dagger on the table and threw myself at him.

The first time he'd seen me in these pj's, I was dancing like a fool by myself in the ballroom, pretending I had some unseen courtly suitor bowing to me. And then Bennett had appeared. That was before the Asarum, before we were together, and I couldn't believe how gorgeous he was, how nervous and excited he'd made me feel. Then he'd danced with me. It had been romantic and sexy, and now I couldn't believe that I got to kiss him and have him tell me he loved me.

"I didn't know it was you," I said. "I didn't recognize your writing. I've seen it before, I should've—"

He showed me his hand in the moonlight. Constant

tremors ran through his fingers and goosefleshed his arm. "My handwriting's changed."

"Oh, Bennett." I felt helpless to do anything, and worried this wasn't the only way the Asarum was affecting him.

"Yeah, forget my dream of becoming a neurosurgeon."

I didn't smile. "Any other side effects?"

He glanced away. "Just the jitters."

"Please don't lie. Not to me. I'm not your parents."

He exhaled. "You're right. Sorry. What else? Well, I can't sleep, I feel like I'm mainlining cappuccino. And I've got no appetite."

"That's it?"

He shot me a wicked grin. "I'm also not sure if I'm thinking clearly—or if that's just being next to *you*. I'm going back tonight, Em. I wanted to say good-bye." He ran a finger along the back of my neck. "And hopefully not be interrupted this time."

"They wanted me to go with you, you know. To the Knell."

He nodded. "Simon told me."

I tried to gauge his reaction. "You don't seem upset that I'm not going."

"You have a life here. School and friends and—you're happy here. The Knell is a graveyard."

"You don't want me to come, do you?" I stepped back, and he reluctantly let his arm drop. "I thought you'd be disappointed, but you don't even want me there."

"Emma." He took a deep breath. "I want you all the time. To hear your voice and see you smile, to touch you." He interlaced his fingers with mine and pulled me closer. "But look at me; I can't keep this up much longer. We need to find Neos and finish him. I need to be at the Knell, doing . . . what I'm doing. And you need to stay here and find that ghost that looks like Rachel."

"Okay." I ran a finger along his breastbone, exposed by the open neck of his blue linen shirt. "I'm sorry."

He grinned down at me. "Don't pretend you were going to go to New York anyway."

"No," I admitted. "I just wanted you to want me to."

"I always want you."

I smiled, but couldn't shake my fears. What would happen when we finally found Neos? I couldn't help wondering if I was strong enough to beat him. Those visions I was having worried me. What if he was already controlling me somehow, the way he had with the siren? I was beginning to wonder if I could trust myself.

I hugged Bennett, feeling the bones and muscles of his back, knowing he'd help me all he could, that I could trust him no matter what visions Neos sent my way, but I stressed over how much Asarum he was taking and whether or not he'd be able to kick it when this was over.

Outside, fat snowflakes dusted the glass ceiling of the solarium. "It's snowing again," I said miserably.

"We call that 'winter,' California girl."

I made a discontented noise as I laid my head against his chest and closed my eyes.

"You're sleepy," he said.

I nodded. "But I don't want you to go. Tell me again about summer. And your boat."

We sat on the wicker couch with the blue and white cushions, and as I curled up next to him, he began to talk in a quiet, lulling tone. That was one of the things I loved most about him, the sound of his low voice. "We'll sail out to this cove I know, just you and me and the wind and the waves. Drop anchor and swim to shore. The beach is sandy, and you can bodysurf or sunbathe. I found a starfish there once, a sort of purple-blue one; I still have it . . ."

I fell asleep like that, my head in his lap, as he told me about all the places he wanted to take me. How hot the sun was, and cold and blue the water. And how we would finally be free. Together.

When I woke in the morning, I was still there, a pillow under my head and a white down quilt covering me. Bennett was gone, but I still felt like I was bobbing in the boat, watching the sun glint off the crystal-clear water.

"You can still come with us," my mother said a couple of hours later. "It's not too late."

We stood in the gravel drive as my dad lugged their bags to the rental car. It reminded me of saying good-bye to them at the airport back in San Francisco, before this whole thing with Neos had begun. Only this time I was dressed warmly enough, because my mother had bought me a coat.

One thing I never gave my mom enough credit for: we may have disagreed about how I should cut my hair, but she totally got what I liked to wear. The jacket was steel-gray wool, cut in a hip-length military style with cool embroidered patches on the sleeve and one shoulder, and lined with thick black sheeplike fleece.

"I'm good." I kissed her before she got into the car. "Thanks again for the coat. I love it."

"You should," Dad said. "She spent long enough shopping for it."

"You have to get the right thing for Emma." She nodded toward my favorite black boots, which she'd also picked out for me. "Because she wears it every day."

My father laid a hand on my shoulder. "I want to tell you to stay out of trouble, but the trouble always finds you, doesn't it?"

"Yeah."

He pulled me into a bear hug. "Just stay safe. I love you."

"I love you, too," I said, and kissed his scruffy beard.

I watched them drive away, feeling sad and alone. I was glad they understood my need to be here, to find Rachel's ghost, to protect my friends, but they never seemed to get that I needed them, too.

I spent the next few days avoiding the Sterns, figuring the best way to stay on good terms with them was to never actually talk to them again. I hadn't figured out my next move, how to find Rachel's ghost, discover Neos's latest plan, or delve further into why I was having visions and nightmares of the smoky snake man. I needed help, but with Simon and Bennett gone, along with my parents, I wasn't exactly sure where to turn.

So I spent the rest of winter break missing Bennett. When I wasn't devouring all the books on his bookshelf, I plinked at the piano in the ballroom, hoping for the Rake, but he never came, and I didn't like summoning him unless I really needed to. Maybe he was withdrawing a little—I didn't know why, but I was trying not to be too needy. Instead I had spontaneous dance parties with Natalie in her bedroom, and Lukas had dragged his Xbox back from his parents' house—we killed more than our share of hours and mutant zombies.

Then there were the marathon movie sessions in the media room at Harry's house. Sara was into some crazy Rule of Three, so we watched the *Spider-Man* trilogy, made fun of the special effects in the first *Star Wars* series, and sat through over nine hours of *Lord of the Rings*, during which Lukas and Natalie would not stop teasing me about my own "precious"—Emma's ring I wore around my neck. While watching the *Twilight* films, our conversation turned philosophical. If there were ghosts and secret ghostkeepers, was it possible there were vampires and werewolves?

Nah.

One sunny afternoon, after yet another heavy snow, Harry's mom scolded us for watching too many movies and told us to "go outside and play," as though we were eight-year-olds. So we built a snow-Gollum in the massive front garden and engaged in a full-on snowball war, vampire girls against Jedi boys. The vampires were winning, of course, when Coby showed up at our flank and started pelting us.

Cheater! I yelled at him.

What? Boys against girls, he said. *Just because I'm a ghost doesn't mean I'm not a guy.*

He grabbed an armload of snow and flipped to the top of the high stone wall surrounding the garden. He made a dozen snowballs and blasted us; one big juicy snowball knocked Sara in the side of the head.

"Coby!" she called, and fired a few balls toward the wall. She actually would've hit him, too, if he hadn't been a ghost. "Can't you do something about him, Emma?"

I was amazed by how comfortable she and Harry were with Coby; sure, they couldn't see or hear him, but that didn't seem to faze them much.

"I can, and I will," I told her. I focused on Coby. *You're going to be sorry you messed with us.*

He laughed and struck me right in the chest with a snowball.

"Ow!" *That's it!* I told him. And I compelled him to keep his hands glued to his sides.

Coby glared at me. *Emma! Who's the cheater now?*

I grinned. *What we girls lack in physical strength, we make up for with other talents.* Except I spoke too soon. Because with me distracted by Coby, Harry and Lukas were down to two-on-two and finally able to beat the others.

Harry shouted something about how beauty always triumphs over brawn, then tackled Sara into a snowbank. Then Lukas did the same thing to Natalie, only he was gentler and less brotherly about it.

Feeling a little left out, I removed my "precious" from my neck and slipped it onto my finger. When I turned into a ghost, I took a big jump and landed sloppily next to Coby on the stone wall.

You're not getting any better at that, he said.

No, I admitted. I didn't say more, because when I wore Emma's ring, I sometimes got distracted by her memories and confused about how I really felt about things. Still, I laughed as I watched my friends playing in the snow, then glanced out over the harbor, just visible between the houses and leafless trees. I felt an intense love for the village across the way; I didn't know if it was Emma's feeling about Echo Point or my own.

I held Coby's hand, and while it didn't feel the same as it would if he weren't a ghost, it was better than not touching, or getting burned. I'd made the right choice, staying here instead of going to New York with my parents and Bennett. All I knew was that I was happy here.

And I wanted that happiness to last. Which meant finding the ghost who looked like Rachel, not having snowball fights with my friends.

What's wrong? Coby asked.

I saw a ghost, I told him. *She looked like my aunt, but I'm afraid she's something else. Maybe one of Neos's creatures, like the siren. And I think she's the key to whatever he has planned next.*

Coby squeezed my hand. *I'll help you find her.*

I squeezed back. *I was hoping you'd say that.*

Oh, and I've been meaning to give you something.

What? I asked.

This, he said, and tackled me from the stone wall into a wet pile of snow.

The next day, Coby and I followed Harry's break-in instructions to the letter and spent the afternoon wandering Thatcher's grounds. We'd split the school in half, and I was checking classrooms, lounges, and the cafeteria, while he hit the libraries and the old servants' quarters.

As I passed through the front hall, I noticed the giant silk floral arrangement someone had donated. Harry had mentioned it when he told us how to switch off the alarm. "That new huge ugly bouquet? I could do something with that." There had been an evil glint in his eye as he planned his next prank. But as I took in the fake gladiolas and long-stemmed roses, I couldn't figure out what he'd do. Although, the black vase did look big enough to hold a few baby pigs—a bouquet of pigs. I smiled at the idea.

It was my first and last smile of the day, because even though I felt the traces of ghosts extending back for centuries, I didn't find any who resembled Rachel. I did, however, manage to summon the ghost jocks as I entered the gym. Actually, it looked more like they'd been waiting for me. They were playing one-on-one, and as I stepped onto the court, Craven bounced the basketball off my head.

"Ow!"

Score! Moorehead called.

Gah! I rubbed my forehead. *Can't you guys* ever *give me a break?*

You want to break? Craven threw himself to the ground and spun around on his back, while Moorehead performed the robot.

You so *died in the '80s*, I told them. I don't know if it was them or the ball, but I was getting a headache. Or maybe I'd been concentrating too hard on summoning. *Have either of you seen a ghost that doesn't belong here? A woman or something else? I don't know, anything out of the ordinary?*

Well, this emo ghostkeeper chick has been stalking us, Craven said, eyeing me meaningfully.

I'm not emo! How do you even know the word? Shouldn't you say, like, "groovy" or "far out" or something?

Coby entered behind me, saying, *Nothing in the staff room*. He caught sight of the ghost jocks. *Hey, what's up?*

Your girlfriend's angst is up, Craven said.

Moorehead nodded. *And the stick.*

Which stick is that? Craven asked, with exaggerated politeness.

The one that's up her—

O-kay! I kicked the basketball at Moorehead, adding a

little compelling force so he'd feel it when it smacked him in the chest, and stalked away.

Coby followed, looking amused, but he didn't say anything as we continued searching, checking the locker rooms, teachers' lounge, and maintenance room. We stopped periodically as I tried to summon the Rachel-looking ghost, but I couldn't feel her in the Beyond.

She's probably hiding, Coby said, as we stepped back into the main hall. *There are some pretty remote places in the Beyond.*

Maybe, I said, crossing toward the door. *Or maybe I only imagined her in the first place.*

Coby, as always, knew exactly what I was thinking. *You don't believe that.*

No. But what am I supposed to do? I can't summon her, so that's that.

What about the ring? he asked. *Why can't you use that to go into the Beyond?*

Because I don't know how. Maybe Simon could . . . wait. I thought about how Simon realized we could reverse-engineer our powers. *What if instead of trying to summon her, I send something to her?*

What? Some kind of message? Coby asked.

Yeah. I closed my eyes, concentrating on my summoning powers, pulling them forth until I could feel a glowing ball in my chest. I infused the ball with a demand, part communication and part compelling force—*come to me.* Then I thought of Rachel, as I'd first seen her at the Knell and as the ghost that appeared outside my window, and instead of pulling that ghost from the Beyond toward me, I pushed the ball of power into the Beyond, toward her.

I was breathing heavily and felt a little faint when I'd finished.

I hope that works, I told Coby, because I didn't know what else to do.

6

I always thought if I had a boyfriend on New Year's Eve, then it wouldn't suck. It wouldn't matter that I didn't have the perfect party to go to, or the right outfit, or that my parents wanted me home *before* midnight. So here I was, finally with a boyfriend on New Year's Eve—only he wasn't here, so it still kind of sucked. Plus, I'd spent a totally frustrating day trying to find a ghost that maybe didn't exist, and got no closer to Neos.

On the other hand, I did have a perfect bash to go to—at Harry's house. And Sara was loaning me something to wear, and the Sterns said we didn't have to be home until 1:00. So maybe I could forget about Neos for one night. And just because Bennett wasn't here didn't mean I couldn't have fun without him.

So Lukas, Natalie, and I got ready to leave the house around 9:00 p.m., just as the Sterns were heading upstairs to bed.

"Emma," Mr. Stern said from the top of the stairs. "I know all about the Armitage boy's parties. Bennett was involved with his sister."

"Uh-huh." Was there a point in there, other than reminding me about Bennett's ex-girlfriend, who they probably liked a lot better than me?

"We're counting on you not to drink and drive," Mrs. Stern explained. She tended to be less opaque than Mr. Stern.

"Oh, of course not!" I widened my eyes and lied through my teeth. "I'm not even sure there's going to be alcohol. Or anything else."

Mr. Stern raised an eyebrow, clearly not buying the wide-eyed expression. It didn't help that Natalie and Lukas were snorting behind me.

"Well," I said, "Harry's not drinking, so I won't, either."

"Thank you, Emma," Mrs. Stern said, though they both stood there looking hesitant to let us go.

"No problem." And I roughly shoved Natalie and Lukas out the front door before the Sterns could change their minds.

"Do you think this is Simon's idea of a joke?" Natalie asked as we piled into the electric blue Yaris.

"Maybe." I got behind the wheel. Simon knew we were embarrassed to be seen in this ridiculous car by other Thatcher kids. So, of course, he'd left it for us.

"Either that, or he meant it as a life lesson. Probably a little of both."

"Hey, stop complaining." Lukas cranked the stereo. "At least now we can listen to our own tunes."

We wound through Echo Point's narrow village streets, then took the left on Ocean that led to the Neck, the even swankier part of town. Harry's driveway was already overflowing, so we parked in front of someone else's castle and walked the two blocks back. Inside we found Harry and Sara at the espresso machine.

"I love your coat," Sara said when she spotted me. "Very Gwen Stefani."

"Thanks." I removed it to show her the black dress, short and tight with a high neck and three-quarter sleeves. "And the dress?"

"Very Sara Watson." Because it belonged to her. She was wearing a long glittery burgundy top over black leggings and chunky heels.

"Except the boots," Harry interjected. "I still say you're hiding cankles."

Sara rolled her eyes. "Harry."

"Do I need to prove it to you?" I stepped out of my boots and kicked one tight-clad leg at Harry.

He grabbed my foot and examined my ankle. "Finely turned," he admitted.

"Thank you."

"Pity about your toes."

"What?" I pulled my foot from his hand, then noticed the glint in his eyes. "Oh, shut up. I'm not falling for it."

"I'm surprised you don't fall more often with toes like that," he mused.

I slipped my foot back into my boot, the better to kick him with. "Harry—"

Sara cut in. "Isn't Harry looking better?"

"For a demon," I muttered.

But it was true. He'd gained some weight since rehab and looked almost European in his diagonally knit gray sweater and narrow-legged black pants.

"Shall I tell you the secret of my restored health?" he asked. "Stop pouring the liter of vodka into your body every day, and you'll stop looking like death."

"Speaking of death," Sara said, "Coby's not here, is he? I can usually tell."

"Not yet," I said, glancing around.

The kitchen was as big as most living rooms, with a Sub-Zero fridge, huge Aga range, and a rustic kitchen table that sat eight. The keg stood behind the island, with a couple of football players manning the pump.

"Are you joining us or them?" Harry nodded toward Lukas and Natalie, standing in line for the keg.

Even from across the room I could tell Natalie was flirting, her head tilted toward Lukas, a naughty glint in her eyes. Lukas had dressed up—for him, anyway—in a black long-sleeved polo and jeans, and Natalie wore a tight, dark-purple silk T-shirt with a cool chunky necklace over a black miniskirt and her leopard-print flats. Though I worried about them being together, I had to admit they'd make a gorgeous couple.

"We got you chai mix," Sara told me. Her back was to Natalie and Lukas, as though she was trying to ignore the flirting.

"You did? That's sweet. But you know what? I want to see how many espressos I can do."

"I can drink you under the table any day." Harry grinned and handed me a shot.

"I don't doubt that for a second." I downed the shot, shivering at the bitter taste. "But it'll still be fun."

The three of us took turns filling and running the machine. After the third shot my stomach began to hurt, and by the fourth I was getting a pleasant buzz. Sara and I were giggling over some raunchy gossip Harry had about a senior girl and freshman boy making out in the pantry, when Coby materialized.

Hey! I said. *Where've you been? I'm so glad to see you!*

He glanced at Harry and Sara. *What've they done to you?*

What? We're having fun.

I've never seen you this cheerful, he said, smiling.

I giggled some more.

"Is that Coby?" Sara asked.

I nodded. It must have looked to them like I was laughing at the refrigerator.

"Why have we never given Emma this much coffee before?" Harry said in Coby's general direction. "She's so much less emo this way."

I stuck my tongue out at him. "I am *not* emo!"

I was about to say more when I heard a guy from my Advanced Bio class yelling something about a blue Yaris.

"Wait, what?"

"You got a blue Yaris?" he asked, making his way toward the keg. "It's about to get towed."

"Where'd you park?" Harry asked.

"In front of that house that looks even more like a castle than this place."

"You're screwed," Sara said. "That guy lives to have people towed."

I shot Coby a panicked look. Two blocks away. There was no way I'd make it in time to stop the tow guy.

I'm on it, he said. *Give me your keys.*

I found my bag and fished for the keys. *Thank you!*

Just stop drinking the coffee. I don't know how to deal with you this happy. Then he disappeared.

I told Harry and Sara that Coby was handling the car situation, then made good on my promise to slow down on the espresso and went outside for fresh air. Everyone from Thatcher was there, and now that I was back in the good graces of Harry and Sara, I was no longer a pariah, which was a relief. I wandered around, joined the dance pit on the patio for a couple of songs, looked for Lukas and Natalie, and stopped to chat with Kylee and another girl from fencing.

That's when Coby reappeared behind Kylee's back. I tried to ignore him, but as he made zombie faces and pretended to bite her neck, I began to snicker. Right in the middle of Kylee explaining she'd been dumped by her boyfriend.

"I'm sorry." I tried to convert the snicker into a sigh.

"That's just so sad." I looked pointedly at Coby. "Guys are such jerks. Go tell Harry to give you one of his special espressos. That'll perk you up."

The excuse to talk to Harry cheered her up, and she and her friend headed toward the kitchen. I found Coby sitting alone in one of the cabanas, watching the kids dancing under the white Christmas lights.

I sidled up and singed him with a little compelling power. Not enough to do any damage, just like a shock from a finger.

Ow!

That was for making me laugh when poor Kylee was telling me about her breakup, I said. *I didn't even know she had a boyfriend.*

It wasn't enough that I saved your car?

You did? How?

Coby grinned wickedly. *I stole the guy's chains, then flashed the lights and honked the horn on his truck, and made the winch go up down. He was a tough old nut, though. He didn't give up until I climbed into your car and drove it away. That freaked him out. I parked in the driveway. No one else saw.*

My hero, I said, laughing. *Again.*

But not really, right?

What? I stopped laughing, not understanding the searching look on his face. *Yeah, really.*

It was always Bennett, wasn't it? Even that night you kissed me.

Oh. *Hero,* as in the romantic lead of my life. I sat on

the lounge next to him, and thought about what I wanted to say.

There's this thing between me and Bennett. I explained about the other Emmas, and the other Bennett—the Rake, and there was probably even one before him. *I don't know, it's like everything I feel for him is wrapped up in those other lifetimes. And now he's taking that stupid Asarum and he's changed. Sometimes I wish he was more like you—that I could trust him, the way that I trust you.*

As a friend.

I guess. I do love you, you know. I touched his arm softly, then moved my hand before I burned it. *It's just different. I'm sorry if you wanted more than I could give.*

He shook his head. *You don't owe me anything, Emma. I just . . . I don't know, I guess I didn't expect to die young. I thought I'd go to med school like my dad, meet some girl, fall in love.* He smiled wryly. *Have more sex.*

My guilt at his death rose like a black wave. I was the reason he'd never go to college, have a career, fall in love, and all the rest. But this wasn't about me; this was about him, so I pushed my guilt aside and listened.

I spend too much time thinking now, he said. *There's not much else to do. Sit around wondering what I could've done with my life, who I could've been. And who I could've been* with. *You, Sara, some girl I hadn't met yet.*

His gaze locked on a cabana across the garden. Natalie and Lukas were lying on their sides in one of the wide lounge chairs, facing each other. He ran his hands through her hair as she traced his lips with her finger, then kissed him.

I guess he'll *never regret not enough sex*, Coby said.

They're not sleeping together, Coby—they're ghostkeepers, they—

Like you and Bennett?

No. Well, yes. But it's completely different.

Sure it is. How could he choose her over Sara? I'm going to check on her, he said, and dematerialized.

I wished I had that ability, instead of being stuck here worrying about Lukas and Natalie. Should I stop them? Warn them about the special hell Bennett and I were stuck in? On the other hand, my mom gave up her powers for my dad, and Bennett's dad gave up his powers for his mom. They all seemed okay.

And I thought about something Sara had said before Coby died. "You can't help who you like." And you certainly didn't want your best friend telling you who you could and couldn't like.

In the end I decided to ignore them and followed Coby into the kitchen to make sure Sara wasn't freaking out. She and Lukas didn't have anything going, but I could tell he'd been on her possibilities list.

I started through one of the sliding glass doors, and felt a faint tug on my senses. A humming in my chest, telling me there was a ghost nearby. Not in our world yet, but in the veil between worlds. I would've ignored the humming, but I couldn't forget what happened the last time I'd been at one of Harry's parties: Natalie had unexpectedly summoned a wraith that I'd barely stopped from tearing into a bunch of kids. I really wasn't in the mood to deal with this, but did I have a choice? So I closed the door and wandered past the patio out to the bluff.

I paused at the edge of the cliff, watching the empty harbor and feeling the weight of the ghost in the Beyond. Not a wraith, but not completely benign, either. My chest tingled as I focused my summoning energy; something felt wrong. This ghost wasn't responding to my summoning. It was coming at me like a guided missile. Denser and stronger than a ghost, and with a keen sense of purpose.

I turned my attention inward, waking my dispelling power, my mouth suddenly dry at the prospect of facing something new and unknown, all alone on the clifftop.

Then she appeared, with a muffled flash of spectral power. She was dressed in a shapeless white gown, her dark hair loose and tangled. When her face came into focus, I gasped and let my power disperse.

Aunt Rachel! Is it—is it really you?

She smiled. *Yes, Emma. It really is. You called?*

It worked? I said in surprise. *I mean, yes, I have questions.*

I don't know how you found me, my dear, but I took pains to ensure that you won't be able to do so again. Her smile skewed slightly.

Why? What are you doing here? You're a ghostkeeper, and I watched that wraith kill you. I'm sorry I wasn't able to stop him. But how could you be a ghost?

Things aren't always as they seem, she said, a pained look in her eyes.

You're not even wearing the same clothing you died in. And she looked a little crazy, but I kept that part to myself. *You were a ghostkeeper, you* can't *be a ghost. Not unless you killed yourself, and—*

She drifted toward me, and her expression changed to pleading. *You have to understand, Emma. I loved Neos. Your mother treated him unfairly. He sacrificed everything for her, and she left him for my brother.*

Yeah, for my dad. *I don't really have a problem with that.*

The Knell refused to help Neos; they hated and hounded him. I thought if I helped him, I could make things right again. I didn't realize he'd changed so much.

He's evil, Rachel.

Is sacrificing for someone you love so evil? she asked. *You are not unfamiliar with a passionate young man who's willing to sacrifice for the one he loves. And I think you're willing to make sacrifices for him.*

My face warmed with anger and I felt dispelling energy crackle along my arms. *Bennett is nothing like Neos!*

She didn't agree or disagree. Instead, she said, *I know the Knell's looking for Neos's ashes. They're at Thatcher.*

What? Why? What are they doing there? How do I find them?

I can't tell you. He'd hurt me if he knew I'd revealed even this much to you. She twitched, as though pulled by an invisible string. *He's looking for me. I must go.*

"No. Wait!" I said aloud. "Rachel!"

I half closed my eyes and drew my summoning energy into my hands, a hard knot of power, then sent tendrils through the veil into the Beyond, to catch Rachel and drag her back into this world. I needed answers. How was she a ghost? What did she know about Neos's ashes, and whose side was she on?

But she didn't reappear, and I couldn't find her. I didn't know how she vanished so completely, but I sent another ball of power after her, just in case, then let my summoning energy dissipate. I stood on the clifftop, letting the chilly air clear my mind, yet I couldn't make sense of what had just happened. I needed to talk to someone, and thought about finding Coby, but realized he wasn't the one I wanted.

I dialed Bennett, and he answered on the first ring. "Happy New Year, Emma."

I smiled at the warmth in his voice. "Happy New Year."

"Is that music in the background? Are you at some club, surrounded by guys?"

"Close. I'm at Harry's, surrounded by chilly clifftop."

"Well, I'm pacing outside Simon's office all alone, so that sounds pretty good."

"I miss you," I said, aching for him.

"Me, too. Next year, we'll kiss at midnight."

"You promise?"

"Yeah, and not just on New Year's. Every midnight for a year." Then his voice changed a little. "What's up? You sound a little—"

"I just saw Rachel. It's her, Bennett, not some shape-shifting ghost. She was too *Rachel* to be anyone else. I know it's impossible, but it's her."

"Another ghost at Harry's?" But he didn't argue with me about her identity, which I appreciated. "The veil must be thin there—either that, or ghosts really like his parties. What'd she say?"

"That she loved Neos, and . . ." I shivered, and not just from the wind. "Oh my God. I know what happened to her, Bennett. I know how she became a ghost. She *allowed* that wraith to possess her, knowing it would kill her. Technically, that'd be suicide, right?"

"Yeah," he said slowly. "Yeah, that makes sense. You think she loved Neos that much?"

"Well, she hated the Knell for turning their backs on him. And she talked a lot about sacrificing for people you loved."

Bennett grunted. "If she's another ghostkeeper suicide, that means she's going to start losing her mind. How'd she seem?"

"Crazy, like Ophelia in *Hamlet*."

"Emma—a Shakespeare reference? Did you get that from Harry?"

"Hey, I know the classics," I protested.

Bennett recited, " 'White her shroud with the mountain snow, larded with sweet flowers, something something the grave did go, with true-love showers.' *Hamlet*. Act three or four, scene something."

Hearing his deep voice reciting some ancient drama eased my fears, and I smiled. "Show-off. Is that how you woo the girls?"

"There's only one girl I care about wooing."

"Well, it's working. But Bennett, she told me something else. Neos's ashes are here. They're at Thatcher." The Knell had been searching for them ever since Rachel had been killed in that first attack. Simon had agreed with Yoshiro that they were the key to dispelling Neos.

"She said that?" he asked. "Do you believe her?"

"I do," I said. "It fits with that smoky vision I had. The stink of ashes."

"Wait—what vision?"

"Oh." I still hadn't told him. "It happened when I was searching the school for her." I explained, but left out his part in it.

"Smoky-snake guy. That doesn't sound good. Did she tell you where his ashes are?"

"She disappeared before I could ask; she said Neos was hunting for her. I couldn't summon her, I guess because she's a ghostkeeper ghost, not a regular one. And I've got this shivery feeling that she and Neos are still connected. I know she still loves him, but maybe she's also afraid, because he's so . . . pyscho."

For a moment, Bennett didn't say anything. I wanted to tell him what Rachel had said about sacrifice, what she'd implied about him following in Neos's footsteps. But I didn't want to be hurtful, or have him think I'd lost faith in him—or in us.

"You know we'll have to dispel her, right?" he finally said, gently.

"I know," I replied. "But if you're forced to kill your own aunt, shouldn't once be enough?"

7

School started the Monday after New Year's, and I sat across from Lukas and Natalie in the breakfast nook, trying to get them to focus. Not easy, considering they were still coming to terms with hooking up at Harry's party.

Were they a couple? Were they not a couple? They weren't quite sure, and seemed to think that gazing at each other soulfully and speaking in double entendres was the best way to find out.

But I had other things on my mind. I ran down the whole thing with Rachel again, and finished with, "So we don't know why Neos's ashes are there, but we have to find them. They must be the key to dispelling him."

I might as well have been talking to myself. Natalie was trying to nibble her toast in a suggestive fashion, while Lukas kept reaching across the table to brush invisible crumbs from her sleeve.

"And that's not all," I continued. "Sara and Harry got together last night."

It took a second for that to sink in, then Natalie snapped out of the daze. "What? *No*! Really?"

"No," I said. "I just wanted your attention. You two are making me sick. Remember Neos? We have to find his ashes."

"We know," Lukas said. "You've told us a hundred times. Can't you just use your reading powers to find them?"

"I'll try, but it hasn't worked yet." I turned to Natalie. "So you'll help me search, right?"

"Oh Emma," Natalie whined. "This early in the morning? Isn't it, like, still the holiday?"

I checked my phone. "You have thirty-two minutes before school starts. Besides, haven't you heard, 'Death doesn't take a holiday'?"

"Is that like a poem or something?" Lukas asked. "Where have I heard that before?"

"I don't know," I admitted. "It might be a mystery novel. The point is—"

"Yeah, we know," Lukas said. "Find Neos's ashes. Got it."

I turned to Natalie. "Fine," she said.

Then Anatole set plates before them and they went back to gazing at each other over their eggs, while I worried about them shutting me out. We'd only lost Simon, but without him, our team seemed to be falling apart, just when I needed them most.

"Emma . . ."

The test prep notes on the board in AP Biology outlined

the functions of the eye. I really needed to focus if I wanted to swing my usual B, but instead I spent the first twenty minutes of class worrying about how I was going to search Thatcher.

"Emma . . ."

The school wasn't that big, but it was full of nooks and crannies, staircases and alcoves, classrooms, offices, and mazelike corridors. I didn't even know what to be looking for. Would they be in some kind of urn?

"Emma!"

I jerked in surprise, realizing that I'd heard someone whispering my name twice already. I turned toward the door and discovered my brother Max, waving frantically at me from the hallway. There had been nothing subtle about his final whisper, and he now had the attention of the entire class and the teacher, Ms. Braby, who cleared her throat and repeated my name. "Emma?"

"That—that's my brother," I stammered. "I don't know what he's doing here."

Max stepped into the room, slightly out of breath, his dirty-blond hair mussed, wearing skinny jeans and a black fleece hoodie. "Sorry, don't mean to interrupt. Family emergency. I need Emma."

"Do you have a pass?" Ms. Braby asked blandly.

"Um—did I not say emergency?" Max answered. "Emma, get your stuff."

I shoved everything into my bag and scrambled toward the door. What the hell was Max doing here? Had something happened to our parents? Was it Neos?

"I'll need a written excuse tomorrow, Emma," Ms. Braby called after me.

I nodded blankly as the classroom door slammed behind me, then followed Max, who was already running down the hall. "Max, wait," I called, as he rounded the corner.

"No time! C'mon, Emma."

"What's happened?" I asked. "Is everyone okay? What are you doing here?"

"Everyone's fine. I'm searching for the ashes, obviously."

"Oh, obviously," I said, not bothering to mask the sarcasm. Figures he'd be ahead of me. I hadn't even started searching yet. Once my parents had filled him in, he'd probably decided to turn this into a competition.

Halfway down the next hallway, he entered a dinky deserted classroom with a cluster of student desks shoved in one corner. Max immediately crossed the floor and opened another door, revealing a seriously decaying staircase leading downward.

"You—" I didn't know where to start. The jamb was shattered. "Did you break the door?"

"Didn't have the key," he explained. "And we need those ashes."

"Really? I didn't know, because while you've been fighting Neos, I've been lazing on the beach in—" I stopped as a thought occurred to me. "Wait, did you find them?" Honestly, I didn't care who found them. I just wanted this to be over.

"Nope," he said, heading down the dark-shrouded stairs. "I found a ghast. You coming?"

I grunted and followed. The walls were built of flaking horsehair plaster and I smelled cool, dank air. The stairs were thick uneven boards, covered in dust and mouse droppings, and cobwebs were impressively, repulsively, everywhere.

"What do you need me for?" I asked. "You're supposed to be a badass compeller."

"It's nasty. Worst ghast I've seen in a long time. I can make it leave me alone for a minute, but I need you to dispel it so we can search this part of the cellar."

"Is it weird to you that we're talking about ghosts?" I asked, brushing cobwebs from my face. He'd kept my parents' secret about me being a ghostkeeper all these years, and I wasn't about to forgive him. "You could've told me, you know. You didn't have to—"

"Emma!" he said, in that irritating tone he always used when I was bugging him. "We can delve into your deep-seated inferiority complex later. Just kill the ghast!"

I made a *hmph*ing noise as I pulled my dagger from my bag and slipped it from its sheath. I couldn't help but be a smidgen smug over the fact Max couldn't dispel a little old ghast.

I took the last step from the stairway onto the dirt floor of the old cellar as Max flicked on a flashlight. The room was low and dark, with empty racks along one of the stone walls and an eye-watering musty smell. A roughly circular stone mound, covered in rotting planks, rose from the gloom at the far end of the room, and I felt my breath catch.

"Is that a grave?" I whispered.

"An old well, I think," Max said, also whispering. "Maybe the original plumbing."

"Oh." I imbued my dagger with power and stepped farther into the cellar. "Well, where's this ghast?"

"Careful," Max warned from the safety of the stairs.

"Why? Because it's *haunted*?" I said, maybe showing just a little more bravado than I felt. But since battling the last ghasts, I'd fought dozens of wraiths, a siren who could control my thoughts, and Neos. I wasn't too concerned. "This is nothing."

"Just summon the damn thing and dispel it already."

"Fine." My boots *were* getting a little filthy from the dirt floor. "Come out, come out, wherever you are," I recited in a sing-song voice.

I sent summoning energy into the void, and it took only a moment for the ghast to appear beside me. Well, not beside me so much as right in my face.

"Whoa!" I backpedaled, almost losing my balance.

It was a woman. I don't know why that surprised me, but it did. She was what I believe they called "strapping" back in the day, about three hundred pounds of fleshy shoulders, wide hips, and tree-trunk legs, with mean eyes and stringy hair pulled into a sloppy bun. I didn't see more after that first glimpse, because before I could dispel her, she swiped at me with one massive paw and I ducked out of the way, narrowly missing the attack.

Surprisingly quick for all that girth, she grinned at me from across the room, next to the old well. Her teeth were all blackened and drool dripped from her mouth, sizzling beneath her. She made a sort of sickening giggly noise that grated along my spine.

"Ooh, boy," I heard Max say behind me. "Not exactly beauty-pageant material. Just dispel her already, Em."

"Jeez, I don't know what I did without your wise advice, Max." My knife tingled with dispelling force; one cut and I'd have her.

I shot the ghast a warning look. *You're not going to make a fool of me in front of my broth—*

She launched herself at me, moving shockingly fast, but instead of burying my dagger in her heart, I only managed to scrape a long furrow down her side. She howled and spun at me as I jumped backward, smacking into the old stone well. I gripped the dagger in my hand, waiting for her to get closer, and felt a sudden surge of energy from across the room. Max was trying to come to my rescue, but he'd only get in my way, so I called, "I got this. Don't interrupt."

"I'm not doing anything."

"You're—"

"Emma, watch out! There's another one!"

As the first one attacked, I leaned back against the well and planted my boots on her belly, driving the dagger like a stake into her heart—then found myself staring into the face of a second ghast, identical to the first, except her stringy hair streamed messily around her pallid face. Hoo boy.

"Twins," Max said. "Sumo ghast *twins*."

I blasted a stream of power at the new ghast, but she was as quick as her sister and dodged almost faster than my eye could follow. I could feel Max unleash his powers as he compelled her to freeze on top of the old well. I clambered onto the rotting planks next to her and slashed her neck with my dagger.

"Die," I said between gritted teeth as I blasted her into vapor with a surge of power.

I stood there for a moment, panting in relief—until the plank sealing the well snapped under my feet. I lunged for safety as the wood tumbled into the well—and heard my dagger *plink, plink, plink* down the stone walls into the dark pool below. It had slipped from my grasp as I'd jumped.

I thought I heard a disembodied giggle echo as the well began to collapse in on itself, sealing my dagger inside.

I stood beside the mound of stones, stunned and breathless.

Behind me, Max said, "Not bad."

"No," I said. "Terrible."

He hadn't seen my dagger fall, and thought I was upset about the fight. "Don't be so hard on yourself." He grinned at my uniform with the plaid skirt. "And since when did we become Catholic? Come give me a hug, Sister Mary."

"You're such a jerk," I said, as he hugged me.

I felt him grin against me. "Some things never change."

But one big thing just had. How was I going to kill Neos without my dagger?

I needed help.

Max had sent me back to class, telling me he'd meet me at the museum later. As I walked through the hallways, I worried about searching Thatcher. Would there be more ghasts waiting for us? Had Neos sent them purposely to get my dagger? No, it had felt like an accident, just stupendously bad luck.

But there were still so many rooms, so many hiding places. I needed someone who knew the school better than I did. So when Harry caught me searching the janitor's room on my way to Trig and said, "Looking to buy the place?" I considered enlisting him. Except the last thing I wanted was to involve Harry with Neos. If he got hurt, I wouldn't be able to live with myself.

I answered, "Not enough closet space," and hurried off to class.

As I waited for Trig to start, I traced the desk graffiti with one finger, then summoned Edmund, the man in the brown suit who'd taught history at Thatcher fifty years ago. He'd been haunting the place ever since, and might know something useful.

Hi, Edmund! I chirped. *How's it going? Any, um, news?*

He eyed me suspiciously. *What do you want?*

Just to chat, I said innocently. *Did you know there were ghasts living in the old cellar?*

I'm dead, young lady, not stupid.

Oh. Well, the reason I was down there is that I need to find Neos's ashes. They're here someplace, I filled him in. *Where do you suppose they could be?*

No, no, no. He shook his head. *I'm not involving myself in any of* that.

Edmund, please. Don't be a wimp. I need your help.

I do not know, he said in his most officious teacher voice, *what gave you any indication that you could speak to me like that, but I'll have you know—*

*I'm sorry, Edmund, you're right. How about this: you help me find Neos's ashes and I'll—*I swallowed. *I'll dispel you.*

He'd been asking me to dispel him since we first met, but I'd refused. Dispelling still felt like murder to me, purely reserved for bad ghosts, or very nasty ghasts. Still, I needed his help, and this was his decision.

Give me your word, he said, knowing I might not follow through without it.

I hesitated. *I—are you sure?*

Positive. He looked completely resolute.

I took a deep breath. This felt so wrong, but with Natalie and Lukas wrapped up in themselves, I needed someone else. And this is what Edmund wanted. *I promise.*

Then we're agreed, he said, almost cheerfully. *But you're quite a powerful ghostkeeper, can't you simply sniff them out? They must reek of Neos.*

I shook my head. *I've tried.*

Ah. Well, perhaps he's found some way to hide the spectral traces of himself. Have you checked the dean's office?

The dean's office was in a little building outside Thatcher's gates. *Hadn't even thought of it*, I admitted.

Hmm. And the attic is a good hiding place, if a bit obvious. Perhaps the old herbal room and the closet under the back stairs? You know, this is quite diverting. I always enjoyed a treasure hunt.

If only we were looking for jewels, I said, thinking of the evil that must fester in Neos's ashes. How was I ever going to defeat him now that I'd lost the dagger?

Edmund waved his hand in the air. *A small matter. There's still my reward.*

I took a circuitous route to the cafeteria, hoping to find some ghostly trace along the way, but all I found was Sara flirting with the two sophomores who'd taken her to Homecoming.

"Isn't it lunchtime?" she asked me.

"Yeah."

"Then what're you doing here?"

"Um, looking for—" I didn't want to tell her about the ashes, either. "You. You ready?"

"Can we come?" one of the guys asked.

"No," Sara told him, then hooked an arm through mine. "Let's go."

As she propelled me down the hall, I glanced over my shoulder. The two boys followed us with their puppy eyes.

"What brought that on?" I asked.

"They're cute."

"Is this about Natalie and Lukas?" I asked worriedly. "Because—"

"I've decided to focus on boys who actually like me, for once," she said, a slight edge in her tone. "Is there anything wrong with that?"

"Not at all," I said. "And they *are* kinda cute. Which one do you like?"

She smiled enigmatically. "Both of them."

We found Harry sitting alone in the cafeteria, poring over a Herman Hesse novel. Natalie and Lukas were M.I.A., and I wasn't sure I really wanted to know what they were poring over.

I plopped down next to Harry. "World Lit?"

"Yeah. Better than *Beowulf*, anyway."

Sara pulled out her panda-bear-shaped bento box and dug into her sushi. A little pretentious, but who was I to talk, with my hand-packed silver and linen? Harry neglected to bring lunch, so I passed him a hunk of fresh-baked bread.

I wanted to tell them about Max and the ghasts, but worried if I told them too much, they'd want to help, and I couldn't risk involving them.

So instead, we discussed Lukas and Natalie hooking up, and while Sara seemed jealous in theory—"because, let's face it, he is really hot"—she didn't seem that upset. Maybe it was her sophomore boys comforting her, or could be she was still hooked on Coby, or she was able to handle rejection well. In any case, I decided I didn't have to worry about her and pressed Harry for better gossip than Lukas and Natalie, mostly because I couldn't figure out how their relationship would end well.

"Did you hear that Britta is dating one of her parents' friends?" he asked.

"No!" I said.

He nodded. "It's true, Monkeytoes. They were seen at—hey!"

The slice of apple I'd flicked bounced off his forehead and fell to the ground. "Do *not* call me that," I said. "There's nothing wrong with my toes."

"Monkeytoes is a term of endearment!" he protested, then his gaze flitted toward the cafeteria doors.

Natalie and Lukas strode in, glowing with happiness.

"God, she looks beautiful," I said.

"She looks happy," Sara said.

"I guess a happy Natalie is a beautiful Natalie," I said. "Not that she was so hard to look at before."

"Yeah," Harry agreed, with an odd look on his face.

Did he actually like Natalie? Great. Something else to worry about. I stuffed an orange slice in my mouth, trying to lose myself in its juicy sweetness.

After school, I waited for Natalie and Lukas at our usual spot at the front gates. I planned on telling them all about Max and the ghasts, but they didn't show. Either they were avoiding me because they knew I'd bug them about finding Neos's ashes, or because I'd reveal my true feelings about two ghostkeepers being involved. Or maybe they didn't want a third wheel—which somehow made me feel worse.

I headed home alone, cursing the icy sidewalks and barren trees. As if I didn't have enough to make me feel crappy, the landscape was positively apocalyptic.

On the other hand, walking into a warm house that smelled of cookies baking wasn't so bad. I rushed into the kitchen and almost ran over a guy carrying a plate of cookies toward the table.

"Max!"

"In the flesh." He popped one of Anatole's cookies into his mouth and sat in the breakfast nook.

Has my brother been bothering you? I asked Anatole and Celeste, who was busy polishing a silver tea set.

Anatole made a disgruntled noise and his mustache bristled. Celeste said simply, *Ah! Thatz who 'e iz. I cannot zay I zee the rezemblence.*

I turned to Max. "What have you been doing to them?"

"So you *can* communicate with them. Mom told me, but . . ." He shrugged as if he couldn't believe it. Probably because he'd always been better than me at everything. And yeah, I resented him a little bit for it.

Max and I did not have one of those perfect sibling relationships. I don't know what it was, but he somehow brought out the worst in me. And the only time he was ever really nice to me was when he was seeing my former best friend, Abby.

Which reminded me. "Why did you dump Abby? You broke her heart."

"I was afraid I'd lose my powers," he protested.

"You idiot—she was weaker, she would've lost *her* powers, not you."

Which she'd done anyway; Bennett absorbed her power after he started taking Asarum. Then I wondered: what was he doing now for power? Hitting up other unsuspecting ghostkeepers? A new worry. They never ended.

"Like you can talk," Max said. "Mom says you're with *Bennett*? I told him to stay away from you."

"Is *that* what you fought about all those years ago?"

"I was protecting you, Emma. Bennett was going to mess you up. You didn't know who you were—you were just a kid. God, you still are. Even if you do kill ghasts."

"Did it occur to you that I might've wanted to know what was going on?" I could feel myself getting angry all over again.

"Mom and Dad said I couldn't tell you. At least I kept Bennett from sucking all your power before you even knew you had any."

"Yeah, well, Mom and Dad are full of crap."

Max started to snap at me, then shook his head. "Damn. I forgot what it was like, having a sister to argue with. I missed you, Em."

And just like that, the steam went out of me. "Me, too. Where've you been all this time? Are you back for good?"

"Until we find Neos's ashes. I'm back enrolled at Harvard. And the Sterns swung me an internship, cataloging the Thatcher archives. That's what I was supposedly doing there this morning. Now have another cookie and tell me everything."

The only "everything" I cared about was the dagger. I explained that it had belonged to the original Emma and I used it to dispel wraiths. "How am I going to kill Neos without it?"

"Can't you use your power normally?"

"Sure, but Neos isn't like other ghosts, Max. I'm not sure if I can beat him *with* the dagger. Without it . . . I don't know."

"We'll figure something out." Max shook his head. "It's embarrassing."

"It was an accident!"

"No," Max replied. "I mean how little I know about you. My baby sister's a living legend, and my best story is about the time she got her butt wedged in a tire-swing," he teased.

"Have I mentioned you're a jerk?"

8

I spent the rest of the week sneaking into offices and rummaging through the hidden hallways from when Thatcher had been Emma's mansion—and, of course, attending the occasional class. Edmund entered wholeheartedly into the spirit of the scavenger hunt, and I hooked him up with Max, so they wouldn't duplicate their efforts. They couldn't communicate, so they did a lot of frustrated miming, which I have to admit I enjoyed watching. Hopefully they'd stumble onto something soon, because I was having no luck myself.

On Thursday morning before school, I knocked on the door of the dean's office inside her little gatehouse building.

"Emma," she said, after opening the door. "Something I can help you with?"

"It's a little embarrassing," I said.

She gestured me into her office. "Come in, have a seat."

I looked at the stack of folders teetering on the chair opposite her desk.

"Ah," she said, making a face. "I'm putting the calendar together. There's Martin Luther King day, teacher workshops, Parents' Night—" She paused, eyeing me. "You didn't know about Parents' Night? Are your folks still away?"

"No." Well, technically they were still *away*, just not missing anymore. But even if they were here, I didn't know if they'd want to go to Parents' Night. I shrugged. "Doesn't matter."

After another moment of scrutiny, she grabbed the folders from the chair and told me to sit. "Now, then. What can I help you with?"

I settled into the chair. "The thing is . . . well, I lost a bet with Harry Armitage. And the loser has to help the janitors after school for a couple days. I thought maybe I could clean this building instead of the main one?"

"So the other students won't see you? I normally frown on betting of that sort," the dean said with a smile. She gestured to her huge pile of files. "But in this case, I'll make an exception."

She said I could come by after school to vacuum, dust, and wipe down the counters in the kitchenette. I thanked her halfheartedly at the door, trying to look abashed, then ran to catch up with Natalie and Lukas at the front gate. When I told them about my clever ploy to search the dean's office, they congratulated me and refused to help.

"This is important," I said. "You're treating it like a

game. Coby's dead, Martha's dead, Bennett's sister, all those other ghostkeepers . . . If we don't stop Neos, more people are going to die."

"Dude," Lukas said, "you're not the only one with a cunning plan. We've spent the whole week sneaking around."

"Yeah, and making out," I muttered.

Natalie grinned wickedly. "It's the perfect excuse! They caught us in the endowment office, but when we started kissing they just thought we were looking for some privacy. They yelled at us, but didn't suspect anything."

"Where are you looking today?" I asked.

"The drama department." Natalie considered. "Lukas is going to dress as a pirate captain."

"I am?" He looked dubious.

"And I'll be your saucy wench."

"In that case," he said, "yo ho ho."

So that afternoon, I swabbed the deck while they . . . well, I didn't know exactly what they did. Probably walked the plank.

I took my time dusting the dean's office, checking all the knickknacks, every cubbyhole and cabinet. As I searched, I couldn't shake the feeling I was being watched. I kept spinning around, expecting to catch someone behind me, but there was no one. Only the weird blond American Girl doll, which for some reason the dean kept on her chair when she wasn't there. After it freaked me out for the third time, I hid it under the desk.

The dean was at a meeting and campus had already cleared out, so maybe it was some ghostly presence making me jumpy. I probed with summoning energy and found nothing but one of Emma's old grooms, only confirming this had once been a carriage house.

I decided it must be the lingering memories of the previous Emma putting me on edge, and went to check the bathroom, which was, of course, empty. A bowl of purple potpourri sat on the toilet, over which hung a bland matching watercolor. The room was totally normal, for a bathroom; there was no reason for my nervousness. Except, as I turned to switch off the light, a hand grabbed my other wrist from behind me.

The Rake would've been seriously disappointed in me. Instead of reflexively striking at a nerve cluster or grabbing the hand and snapping the fingers, I shrieked.

The hand released me. "It's not gold."

It was Britta, my gorgeous, tawny-skinned nemesis—the girl who sat next to me in Western Civ and hogged all the sunlight. Except at the moment she looked more chalky than glowy, nervously checking my hand like she was afraid she'd done damage.

"What?" She was staring at the silver band on my finger Bennett had given me. "What are you doing here?"

"I am doing a research project," she said, like she was reading off a TelePrompTer. "What are you doing?"

"Um. Something for the dean. Are you okay?"

She fidgeted, tugging at her school tie, then rolling her shoulders like her bra was too tight. "I am studying the architecture of the school and grounds."

"Well, good luck with that," I said, putting on my coat.

"Thank you!" Britta said, smiling at me.

Why was she being so nice? I had enough problems, I didn't have time to worry about Britta going off her meds. I mumbled a good-bye and fled for the museum.

The next day, I complained to Edmund about the wild goose chase in the dean's office, but he was so happy poring over antiquarian books with Max that he didn't even take offense. Later, between fifth and sixth period, I snuck into the staff lounge. The walls were lined with bookshelves, and old leather couches and oriental rugs gave the room a clubby feel. Dim light came in through the low curtainless windows that looked over the front gates.

I doubted Neos's ashes would be there, but I had to look even if I didn't know what exactly I was looking for. Could the ashes be buried? Hidden inside a cushion or a wall? How much space did they take? Why couldn't I sense them? The possibilities seemed infinite, and casing the staff lounge made me feel sick to my stomach. I rifled through drawers and files, panicked about coming up with a good excuse if a teacher walked in.

Just as I decided nothing was here, I noticed a file box on a top shelf. I reached up high, and tipped it to the floor. The lid popped off and papers exploded everywhere.

I swore.

"You rang?" Harry stood in the doorway, with Sara behind him.

I stooped to pick up the papers. "What are you guys doing here?"

"We followed you, of course," Sara said, adding some papers to my stack. "You've been acting even freakier than normal, so we wondered what you were up to."

"I have *not* been acting freakier than normal."

"So you admit you normally act freaky?" Harry asked.

"No, I—shut up."

He shoved a bunch of papers onto the stack. "You know, if you take your shoes off, you can use your monkey toes to make this go twice as fast."

"I don't need my feet to strangle you," I said, then asked Sara, "Were you really following me?"

"Kind of. We couldn't figure out who you were sneaking off with," Sara said. "I mean, you're so in love with Bennett. Harry thought maybe a teacher."

"An older man," Harry said, replacing the file box on the shelf. "Like Sakolsky. The girls all love Sakolsky."

"Sakolsky?" I said. "Why not Jones? He's better-looking. Younger, at least. And not a math nerd."

Sakolsky, however, turned out to be a prophetic choice, as he happened to walk in at that moment. "What are you doing here?" he demanded. "You're not allowed in the staff lounge."

"We're looking for you," Sara said. "Emma and I missed tonight's homework assignment." Her lie was so facile I almost believed it, until I remembered I had the assignment written in my notebook.

Sakolsky eyed us, and we all put on innocent expressions, which was more difficult for Harry. He didn't have that kind of face.

"And you?" Sakolsky asked him.

"Would you believe I was just keeping them company?"

"No."

"In that case, they came for their homework, but I'm looking for a place to stash a chimp."

"You have a chimp?"

"Not yet, sir," Harry said. "I haven't found a place to stash him."

Sakolsky started to answer, then shook his head, unwilling to continue the conversation. He opened his briefcase and gave us the assignment, which Sara and I both dutifully marked in our phones.

"Don't let me catch you in here again," Sakolsky said. As detention was the last thing I needed right now, I thanked him profusely and scooted to sixth period, ignoring Harry's and Sara's hints that this wasn't over. I still wasn't sure what to tell them.

The bell rang as I hit my seat. I glanced at Britta, sitting to my right, waiting for the inevitable snarky comment. Then I remembered how strangely she'd acted the day before.

She was smiling at me again. "Just made it," she said, and dorkily pretended to wipe sweat from her brow.

"Yeah," I said, hesitantly.

"Nick of time."

"Uh-huh." I looked at her more closely, and she seemed kind of uncomfortable in her own skin. "Are you okay?"

She fidgeted. "What? Why would you ask that?"

"Because you're acting all nice. What's wrong?"

"Nothing. I am nice."

"Have you *met* you?"

"Girls," Mr. Jones cut in. "If you're done, I'd like to proceed with class. Since you're so talkative, Emma, why don't you tell us what you thought of the reading?"

I felt my face flame, not because Mr. Jones had singled me out, but because I'd told Harry and Sara I thought he was good-looking. Not that he knew I'd said that, but I still felt embarrassed. At least Harry and Sara weren't here to witness it. Harry would've noticed and made some veiled remark.

But as we discussed the French Reformation, I realized it wasn't thinking Mr. Jones was cute that was making me feel funny. My spine tingled, and pressure radiated into my arms. Which could only mean one thing: there was a ghost nearby, one I didn't recognize.

But where? If I stood to summon it, I'd look like a complete freak. I rolled my shoulders, letting my ghostkeeping power flow down my arms into my hands. I adjusted my position in my chair, trying to direct the probing tendrils of my power. I felt the imprint of a ghost thickening the air in the classroom, but couldn't pinpoint its location.

A wraith? I didn't think so, but couldn't be sure. I shifted in my chair, trying for a better position, and Jones said, "Yes, Emma? Do you need to use the bathroom?"

The room filled with laughter. I no longer thought he was cute.

"No," I muttered.

The ghostly energy swirled and shifted. Jones continued with his lecture and Britta gave me a sympathetic look, which further weirded me out.

I scanned the classroom, trying to focus my powers without moving. No luck. The room was typical for Thatcher, and looked more like a drawing room than a classroom, with burnished wood paneling and antique furniture. And plenty of resident ghosts that I was able to ignore—unlike this one. I didn't know why, unless it was Rachel.

An agonizing forty minutes later, the bell finally rang. I was the first one out of the classroom, but I lingered outside the door, waiting for the room to empty. With everyone gone, I could work my magic and summon the ghost. I longed for my dagger, but even if it was a wraith, I should be able to dispel it without help.

Britta stopped and smiled at me. "Are you okay? I'm so mad at those students for laughing at you."

"Yeah, I'm sure you feel terrible."

"Why can't we be friends, Emma? Like those other friends of yours. You know, um—"

"What, Harry and Sara?" She really was acting weird.

"Harry and Sara," she repeated in a robotic voice.

"What the hell is up with you? Are you recording this for some practical joke? Did Harry put you up to this?"

She smiled woodenly and wandered away.

"Okay," I said to nobody in particular, and waited for Mr. Jones to drag his un-cute self out of the classroom.

Then I slipped back inside, pretending I'd left something behind. After I was sure I was alone, I got into my summoning stance and unleashed my full powers, but only felt traces of the unfamiliar ghost, until I heard someone clear his throat.

Jones stood at the door, watching me. "Is that qigong?" he asked.

I felt myself flush. "Tai chi. The beach ball pose." I tossed an imaginary beach ball at him, and scurried away.

I zoned through my last class, too worried about what I'd sensed to concentrate. Was Rachel back? Had she brought Neos with her?

When the final bell rang, campus cleared out quickly. But as I gathered my things from my locker in the Lame Lounge, my spine began to tingle. The ghost was back, and not far off. I exited the lounge and followed its trail to a long corridor that stretched before me, lined by closed doors. It was the music and art department, and since I was skilled at neither, I never came down here. The lights flickered as I walked along the empty hallway, like in some low-budget horror film, and despite the cheesiness, my heart caught.

I needed to remember the lessons the Rake and Simon had taught me. I needed to remember who I was. I wasn't the scared little girl who accidentally blundered into the monster's lair; I was the kick-ass hunter who drove a dagger through its heart. I might have felt braver if I'd actually still had my dagger.

I heard scuffling from inside one of the rooms, then a short, terrified scream and a grunt. There was a clamor of discordant music—piano keys struck randomly, violin strings shrieking and snapping.

Then I heard Sara yelling for help. "Coby! Emma! We need you!"

Lunging across the hallway, I pulled on the knob, but the door wouldn't open. Through the little rectangular window I caught a glimpse of the music room, glowing with a flickering light. Harry and Sara stood back to back, he holding a trumpet and she a chair, as three music stands whirled around them, whipping and slashing with sharp metal edges.

Two of the stands were wielded by a ghost in a 1900s-looking police uniform, and the other by a little rat-faced man. And in the far end of the room was Britta, who actually was floating on her own. Her face was contorted, and her normally tawny skin burned with a dull light. I was terrified for Harry and Sara. How could I have missed what was happening to Britta? She wasn't being nice to me, she was possessed.

A music stand slashed at Harry, and he barely deflected it with his trumpet. Sara yelled, "*Someone*, please help!"

"Where is it?" Britta asked, in an awful gravelly voice that wasn't her own. "Where does she keep it?"

I yanked harder at the doorknob, feeling the beginnings

of panic. Locked tight, the knob wouldn't turn an inch. I couldn't get to them, couldn't save them.

"Screw you," Sara spat. "We'll never tell—"

"Wait, wait!" Harry said desperately, as a music stand barely missed his head. "I'll tell you!"

Britta's voice grew eager, rapacious, and the rat-faced man and the cop held the music stands in the air. "Tell me. Tell me now, or die."

"She threw it into the fire," Harry said, his voice trembling.

"What?" Britta shrieked. "What fire? Where?"

I rammed my shoulder against the door, but it didn't budge. It wasn't locked, it was stuck with ghostly energy.

"Sauron's mountain," Harry said. "After Gandalf told her—"

"You lie!" Britta bellowed.

She hovered directly over Harry, and the other ghosts spun the music stands closer, for killing blows.

Sara screamed again, and I lashed at the door with compelling power and hit it with my shoulder at the same time. The door flung open and I skidded halfway across the floor, but it didn't matter—I didn't need to aim. I loosed a burst of dispelling force strong enough to scour the room of ghosts. The cop and the rat-faced man unraveled into scraps of spectral dust, and the ghost inside Britta vaporized, too.

She dropped from the ceiling directly onto Harry. His trumpet clattered across the floor, and sheet music drifted down around us like snow.

"Damn," Sara said, catching her breath.

"It's over," I said. "Are you guys okay?"

"No!" Harry said, lying in a heap under Britta. "I've got *Paranormal Activity* sitting on my head."

"Poor Britta," I said, rolling her off him. Her skin was already regaining a more natural color, and though she was still unconscious, she seemed to be breathing okay.

"Poor Britta?!" Sara said. "She almost killed us."

"That wasn't her," I explained. "She was possessed."

"Yeah, we noticed," Sara said, her face flushed. "What the hell is going on?"

"Um . . . can you put the chair down?"

She realized she'd been holding the chair like she was preparing to brain me. "Sorry."

Then Lukas burst into the room, followed closely by Natalie. "What happened?"

"A ghost possessed Britta," I said, "and drafted some others to help her threaten Sara and Harry."

"Britta said Emma wanted to meet us here," Harry said, lifting his head from the floor. "She was after your precious."

I touched the chain around my neck, and felt the band of gold still hanging there under my shirt. "My ring?"

"She wanted to know where you kept it," Sara explained.

"How hard is it to find?" Natalie asked.

"Well, she didn't seem like the sharpest ghost in the attic," Harry said, lying back down. "And she sounded like she was from the seventeenth century. Now if you'll excuse me, I need to faint." He held his hand to his head like an old Victorian lady.

"Why did she want your ring?" Lukas asked.

"Ghosts can possess people?" Sara said, panicked. "Can we stop them? How do we stop them? Where's Coby? Why—"

"Slow down!" I told her. "Neos must still want my ring. He thinks it'll have the opposite effect on him and let him become mortal. He's gotten more powerful. He doesn't need the amulet anymore to possess people, and now I guess he's teaching other ghosts how to do it. When I ran into Britta yesterday, she seemed strange. She wasn't possessed by *this* ghost, though; I would've noticed."

"Strange how?" Natalie asked.

"I don't know. Talking weird. And she checked out my hands, like she was . . ." I fingered the silver band on my right hand. "Yeah."

"Looking for your ring," Natalie finished.

"Could she have been possessed by a completely different ghost yesterday?" Lukas shook his head. "We'd better call Simon."

"How'd you find us?" Sara asked Natalie.

"Lukas sensed a major ghost and we came to check it out," Natalie told her.

"Next time," Sara said, "come faster."

"Odd that I didn't notice any . . . ," Natalie mused, then petered off, as though something had just occurred to her.

The same thing was occurring to me. That had been a

serious ghost, plus two more. Why had Lukas sensed the ghost and not Natalie? She was the summoner, more sensitive to ghosts that weren't right in front of her. Which meant it was already happening.

On the floor beside Harry, Britta moaned and started to wake.

"I'll deal with her," Sara said. She helped Britta sit up and began to lie. "Sweetie, did you forget to eat today?"

Britta blinked at her. "W-what?"

"You fainted."

"I don't remember."

"No? We were talking, and—"

"That's not what happened. It was her." She pointed a finger at me, her perfectly manicured nail looking more like a claw. "Emma."

I opened my mouth, not sure what to say, when Lukas crouched beside Britta, his eyes warm and concerned. "Why don't I drive you home?"

The light returned to her eyes, and she said, "Would you?"

He said, "My pleasure," as Natalie rolled her eyes.

"I'll follow you and give you a ride back," Sara said. "Coming, Harry?"

"No." He finally stood. "I want to talk to Emma."

Britta risked one last look at me. "I know you did something. I'm going to get you for this."

"Oh, Britta," Harry said. "You're like the bitchy girl in a bad movie. It's adorable."

She made a strangled sound as Lukas escorted her into

the hallway. Natalie and Sara trailed along behind, leaving me alone with Harry.

"I'd better go," I said. I didn't want to get him more involved in any of this.

"I'll walk you," he replied, his voice determined.

9

"Maybe you should go home and take a nap," I suggested, making one last attempt to avoid a confrontation with Harry. He'd left his car in the lot and followed me out of Thatcher's front gates.

He slipped his arm in mine. "You know better than that. If I was easy to dodge, I'd have no friends."

"Are you kidding? Everyone loves you."

"Well, I *am* irresistible," he allowed. "Like chocolate-covered happiness."

I snorted. "That ghost that possessed Britta wanted to crack open your cream-filled center."

"Doomed to failure. Everyone knows I'm full of nougat."

We waited for a break in traffic, then crossed the street. "What are we talking about, again?" I asked.

"We're talking about killer ghosts hunting you, using your friends as bait."

I swallowed. "I'm sorry. That's why I haven't told you

what's going on. I didn't want to drag you and Sara into this. First Coby, and now—"

"You idiot," he snapped. "I'm not worried about us. I'm worried about *you*. Emma, listen to me. I cannot lose another friend."

"Neither can I, Harry," I said, extricating my arm. "Why do you think I tried to keep you out of this?"

I strode ahead and he struggled to keep up with me. I walked quickly, trying to stay warm, while avoiding the patches of ice along the sidewalk. Harry caught my arm as I almost slipped.

"I can't see ghosts," he said. "I can't shoot death rays from my fingertips and battle wraiths. But I can help, Emma. Me and Sara both."

"No," I said, firmly. "Stay out of it."

"Don't tell me that. We're already in it. Because of Coby, because of you. You're not the only one who wants to avenge Coby, and you need help. Tell me what's going on."

We turned down the museum drive, and I found Coby standing in the middle of the gravel lane, looking like something out of a supernatural thriller. His gorgeous face, the gray suit, the cold New England landscape his backdrop. The museum even looked haunted, which I suppose it was.

He's right, you know, he said. *You should let him help.*

Why? So he can get killed like you?

Because we need all the help we can get. It's time to end this, Emma. I'll protect Harry.

"Coby's here, isn't he?" Harry asked.

I nodded. "He says I should let you help."

"He's pretty smart for being so good-looking," Harry said.

I didn't want to admit it, but Coby was right. With Simon and Bennett gone and Natalie and Lukas busy with each other, I felt rudderless. I needed a new team. Coby, Max, and now Harry and Sara.

"Okay, then." We stood there in the cold in the middle of the museum's driveway while I told him about Aunt Rachel, the Knell, and Neos's ashes.

"Whoa," he said, when I finished. "I can't wait to get all that on Twitter."

"Harry!"

"Kidding. But there's a whole secret society and everything? I guess I thought it was just you, a couple other ghostkeepers, and a few big, bad ghosts."

"That's why I didn't want you involved. It's dangerous, Harry."

He looked toward the snow-covered trees, and I thought he was going to back out, but he said, "I can find the ashes. I spent two semesters stashing bottles at Thatcher—I know every corner and hidey-hole."

Coby grinned. *I told you.*

Maybe it was the ghost that had possessed Britta and almost killed Harry and Sara, or maybe it was just the cold, but I was suddenly overwhelmed. Tears filled my eyes at how grateful I was to have friends like Coby and Harry. They hadn't even known me three months, and now here they were helping me fight for everything.

"Ah, Emma, don't cry," Harry said. "Why are you crying?"

"I don't know," I sniffled.

Coby reached out an arm to comfort me, then remembered he could burn me. His expression, as I flinched away from him, was devastating. I could see in his eyes the hurt and frustration that he was no longer alive. And as Harry put his arms around me, I cried all the harder into his thick wool coat.

Harry and Coby left me at the door, and it was a relief to step into the warm stillness of the museum. I shed my coat and boots in the hall closet and considered my next move.

I wanted to run upstairs and climb into bed. Ask Nicholas to make me a fire, Celeste to bring me hot chocolate, then cry into the phone to Bennett about the possession. But Nicholas was dead, I didn't like ordering Celeste around, and Bennett was too far away to be of real comfort.

I needed to face this head-on. I thought for a second, with one hand on the banister, and a plan took shape in my mind. I went to Mr. Stern's office and knocked on the door. He looked up, his expression vague yet concerned. "Are you all right, Emma?"

"I need to talk to you," I said. "All of you. Mrs. Stern, Lukas, Natalie, and we need Max. Do you have a speakerphone in here? Could we call the Knell that way?"

He pierced me with those blue eyes that were so much like Bennett's. "What's this about? What's happened?"

"A ghost possessed a girl at school."

His breath caught. "A regular ghost? An ordinary girl? I mean, not a wraith and not a ghostkeeper?"

"Yeah. But I only want to tell the story once, if that's okay."

He nodded. "Of course, Emma. I'll let them know at the Knell and tell Alex. You really are all right?"

I nodded. "Just shaken up."

"I can imagine," he said, with an absent smile. "Well, you're not the only one, but we'll get through this."

I nodded, then went to the kitchen, where I politely asked Anatole to make me a mocha red-eye chai.

Rough day? he asked, sliding it along the counter toward me. The American idiom sounded funny coming from him.

And it's only going to get worse, I said, anticipating my parents and Bennett's reaction when I told them that Thatcher students were getting possessed. And that Neos was after my ring.

We all gathered in Mr. Stern's office—me, Lukas and Natalie, and Mr. and Mrs. Stern. Max had been the last to show, and was bitter about cutting his Ancient Greek class. Mr. Stern dialed the Knell.

Simon's voice came from the speakerphone. "Whenever you're ready, Emma."

"Is Bennett there?" I asked.

"No, he's—out at the moment. But please, go ahead."

"We're here, honey," my father said, from the speaker.

I wanted to ask Simon about Bennett, but couldn't, not with his parents sitting there. So I just told them what happened. "Then Sara called and told me that Britta seems fine," I finished. "She stayed with her after Lukas dropped them off."

"Why didn't you stay, Lukas?" Simon asked. "Sara can't detect spectral activity."

"I wouldn't let him," Natalie said. "Have you *seen* Britta?"

Mr. Stern shot her a look. "I'm sure we can all trust each other here."

"I trust Lukas with my life," Natalie said. "Just not with Britta's pants."

"Natalie!" Mrs. Stern said sharply, and Natalie had the grace to look embarrassed.

I glanced at Lukas and saw him slouch in his seat, inspecting his phone with great fascination.

"And the girl," Simon said, ignoring them. "Britta. She has no memory of the possession?"

"I don't think so. Sara says Britta thinks *I* did something to her. We're not exactly friends," I admitted.

"If you could overnight an item of clothing she was wearing," my father said, "I'll read it and try to learn more."

"How are we supposed to get her out of her clothes?" I asked.

"Not a problem," Lukas murmured, so only Natalie and I could hear.

Natalie elbowed him, and I spoke before they had a chance to start bickering. "She doesn't remember exactly what happened, but what if she knows, on some level, that I was the target?"

"Which is why your father and I have decided you're not safe there," my mother said. "We think you should come to New York." She started listing all the reasons I'd be safer with them, treating me like a twelve-year-old.

To my surprise, Max came to my defense. "Mom—she's fine. They don't call her Emma F. Vaile for nothing."

"She is not Emma *F.* Vaile; you should know your own sister's middle name," Mom scolded.

"The 'F' is for . . . Frickin'. She's Emma Frickin' Vaile, Mom. She battled Neos to a standstill *twice*, and now you rag on her?"

My parents seemed to realize their hypocrisy and settled down. I was glad Max was on my side.

Then Simon gave us a rundown of his thinking about the theory and practice of possession. "Ghosts possessing the living are dangerous to others—as Harry and Sara can attest—but also to the host. If Emma hadn't dispelled that ghost, the girl at school could've suffered lasting damage."

"This is so the 'Charlie's Angels' episode of *Supernatural*," Natalie whispered to me as Simon droned on the speakerphone. Mrs. Stern gave us the eye from her chair. I tried not to prove that I was a twelve-year-old by snickering and giggling, and instead pressed my arm against Natalie's to let her know I thought it was funny. It reminded me how much I'd missed her since she'd hooked up with Lukas.

"I still don't understand why he possessed a student at Thatcher," Mr. Stern said. "Why not just go after Emma himself? And why does he need the ring?"

"We don't know what kind of shape he's in," Simon said. "He could just be experimenting."

"Experimenting?" Mrs. Stern asked. "To what end?"

"I presume he's searching for a permanent body for himself," Simon answered.

"Ew." Natalie made a face. "Britta crossed with Neos? Now there's a nightmare I hadn't considered."

"Not Britta," Simon's voice said over the speaker. "A ghostkeeper. A powerful ghostkeeper. With whom he already shares a connection."

All eyes in the room turned toward me. I even felt my parents' and Simon's eyes boring into me through the phone.

"Maybe he's just after the ring." I couldn't bear the thought of Neos possessing me. "He's always wanted it. He hopes it'll have the opposite effect on him, make him mortal. I don't know, maybe he thinks I'm part of that equation. But right now, we need to focus on protecting the kids at Thatcher."

"And the teachers," Lukas somewhat reluctantly added.

"We have to focus," Simon corrected us, "on finding

those ashes, and understanding Neos's plan. We need to learn to anticipate him. I suspect Neos is setting the stage for another confrontation. One designed to guarantee him victory."

A silence fell. We were stuck *responding* to Neos all the time, trapped on his chessboard like pawns. I was ready for a different game.

"I'm going to use my ring to find the ashes," I said into the silence. "I'll search as a ghost. I can look between the walls, inside furniture. Nothing will be closed to me. I can even check the original Emma's memories for hiding spots."

"I'm not sure that's wise," Simon said.

"Why not?"

Mrs. Stern answered. "Maybe Neos drew your attention to the ring because he *wants* you to flit around Thatcher like a ghost."

"Precisely," Simon said. "Wearing the ring makes you a ghost, which might make you vulnerable to him. And why haven't you been able to sense his ashes? You're the strongest reader we have. If he's able to hide *them* from you, what else is he hiding?"

"Well, we have to do *something*," Natalie said. "We can't rule out everything because maybe that freaking wraith-hole *wants* us to do it."

Simon coughed—possibly covering a laugh at "freaking wraith-hole." "That's also a good point. Perhaps Emma *should* search as a ghost . . . but not alone. The only other person who can stand against Neos for longer than a handful of seconds is Bennett. God knows he doesn't sleep anyway. I'll send him to watch her back."

Simon, my parents, and the Sterns spoke for another ten minutes, but it was basically decided. We'd keep searching for the ashes.

After we ended the conference call, I went straight up to my room to call Simon back in private. "Where is he?"

"I don't know, Emma. He . . . roams."

"He's not a stray dog, Simon."

Simon didn't say anything, but somehow he managed to not say anything really emphatically.

"What?" I demanded. "Just tell me."

"He leaves at night and wanders the city. I honestly don't know if he sleeps anymore. He's mastered the art of seizing other ghostkeepers' power. Asarum opened that door, and he jumped through."

"Where—who is he taking power from?" I felt sick.

"I don't know. I can't talk to him. I have to say his name three times before he hears. He stinks of power, and the Knell ghosts are terrified of him. He's burning himself out, Emma, he's—"

"Stop! Stop, Simon, please. I get it."

More gently, he said, "I'm sorry, Emma. I don't know what kind of game you two are playing, I don't know what secrets you have. But I do know you're playing with fire."

He wouldn't tell me what secrets he meant, and he wouldn't believe that we didn't have any. So I told him about my other problem. "Simon, I lost my dagger."

"I know," he said gloomily. "Max is in touch with your parents. Emma, you can do this. And we're doing everything we can to help you. But be careful."

After we hung up, I called Bennett and left a message, then called him again and left another. Then, lying in bed hours later, I called him a third time. He didn't answer, and he didn't call back.

I wanted to spend the whole next day in bed, waiting for Bennett to call and say he'd guard me while I searched Thatcher in ghostly form. But he didn't call, and his mom—looking as stern as ever, like last night never happened—sent me off to school.

I stumbled through the day, then Harry came home with me to study for a Latin test. He followed me into the kitchen, and I didn't think twice before asking Anatole to brew Harry a pot of strong coffee while I made myself a cup of English Breakfast tea.

"Uh, Emma," Harry said. "I don't want to alarm you, but the coffee seems to be making itself."

I laughed. I was so used to living with ghostkeepers, I'd forgotten I had friends who couldn't even see ghosts. "That's Anatole. He's the resident French chef. You'd like him."

"Oh, yeah?" He grinned. "Got any resident French maids?"

"Actually . . ."

"Tell me you're kidding! A French maid? Does she wear a little skirt and fishnet stockings?"

"She's a real maid, Harry, not a strip-o-gram."

Anatole set a ceramic pot full of coffee and a fresh cup in front of Harry on the counter, then, with a twitch of his mustache, began to pour.

You're enjoying this, aren't you? I said.

Mais oui, Anatole said with a grin. *It iz not often I get to haunt.*

I tried to imagine it from Harry's perspective. "It must look so weird to you."

Harry ran his fingers above the coffee pot as though checking for strings, and his hand passed through Anatole. "Not as weird as your monkey toes."

I sighed and we went into the solarium. The day had been bright and blue, though it got dark at about five, so the sun was already low in the sky, but the room was still warm and full of thriving citrus trees. Anatole really did have a way with them.

We sat next to each other on the blue and white couch, and I was reminded of the last time I'd seen Bennett, how I'd fallen asleep in his lap.

We opened our Latin books and starting gossiping about Sara's "parasophomours" as Harry liked to call them—a mashup of "paramour" and "sophomore."

"She really should just pick one of them," Harry said.

"If she were a guy, would you be saying the same thing?" I asked. "There's always a double standard about that stuff."

"Emma," he said, laying a hand over his heart. "I am nothing if not a romantic."

"Then why don't you have a girl? Or a boy?" Maybe that was why he never had a girlfriend.

"Who am I supposed to go out with? Sara's my best friend and still in love with Coby. Natalie's with Lukas. Plus she's *Natalie*; I'm too devoted to my own self to ever have enough for her."

I giggled. It was true. A narcissist can never have a functioning relationship with another self-absorbed person. "Half the girls in school have crushes on you."

"Or on my money," he said. "Maybe I should go for Britta. She's more interesting since she grew horns and a tail."

"Ugh. I couldn't bear that."

"Then who, Emma? " He considered me. "Bennett's in New York, and he always makes you cry. You aren't really taken, are you?"

A rough voice came from the direction of the kitchen. "Yes. She's taken."

Bennett stood in the doorway, looking pale, red-eyed, and furious. His black long-sleeved T-shirt and jeans hung on his emaciated frame. Even after talking to Simon, I still had hoped that he'd cut down on the Asarum, but instead he'd upped his dose.

"Bennett," I said, cautiously.

"What's going on here?" he demanded.

"What does it look like?" I said, pointing to our Latin texts. "We're studying for a test."

He casually glared at Harry. "Is that how you play it, Armitage?"

Harry didn't back down. He tilted his head and grinned. "Well, it's not my looks she's after."

"I'm not after anything." I jumped up and crossed the room to Bennett. "What is up with you? Harry isn't into me."

"Yeah, I am," Harry piped up. "Who wouldn't be? Am I right, Stern?"

"*Harry!*" I said over my shoulder. "Not helping!"

"Your boyfriend's an addict," he said, dropping his habitual lightness. "Look at him, he's jonesing right now, out of his mind. What's he on?"

"Nothing," I said. "A stupid Chinese herb. It only affects ghostkeepers. Gives them more power."

Harry stepped closer to us. "You feeling strong, Bennett? Ready to beat the world?"

"Get out of my face," Bennett snarled.

"Or what? You're going to hit me?" Harry asked. "You can fool Emma, but you can't fool me. I've been there."

"Harry, shut up!" I said.

And I realized that's what Harry wanted. He wanted to goad Bennett into hitting him. Harry wasn't strong or athletic, but he was smart and brave. He saw that Bennett was an addict and wanted to show me what that meant.

He was trying to protect me by making Bennett beat him up.

I put my hands on Bennett's chest and shoved him away from Harry, into the kitchen. "Stop this right now," I told him. "This isn't you."

"I saw you. You were laughing and—"

"What—I'm not supposed to laugh when you're not here?"

"No." He rubbed a trembling hand over his eyes. "I don't know what I'm saying. I'm so tired."

As we stood there, I felt waves of spectral energy coming off him, building and cresting and crashing across the room. I felt the pulling gravity of his need, of his hunger for power, almost like a—almost like a wraith wanting to feed.

"Go upstairs," I told him. "Wait for me."

He shook his head like he was trying to shake away confusion. "Don't leave me, I can't—"

"I'll be there," I said gently. "I'll be there in a minute."

He pushed through the kitchen door into the hall, and I hoped that he didn't notice Anatole and Celeste flinching from him.

I went back to Harry in the solarium. "I'm sorry about that, but you shouldn't—"

"Don't trust him, Emma. Whatever you think you two have, he's got other needs now."

"No. He's fine—he'll be fine. It's just an herb, Harry, it's not like—"

"Emma, that was hard-core and you know it." He

repacked his Latin text and Droid in his cargo bag and slipped it across his body as he rose. "Just watch yourself, okay?"

"You didn't have to try to get beat up just to show me how bad it is."

"We all have our strengths." He placed his hands palms-together over his chest and said, "Namaste."

That surprised a smile from me. "Oh, shut up."

"I mean it, though," he said, as he headed outside.

I thought about what it meant. "With love." And I was happy to have him as a friend.

10

What's Bennett's favorite food? I asked Anatole. *Something you can whip up really quick?*

Anatole pursed his lips. *Well, there iz beef bourguignon.*

Pfft, Celeste said. *That takez all day to cook.*

He always like ze crepe, Anatole mused.

Oui! Celeste agreed. *With ze chocolat and Cointreau.*

I impatiently watched Celeste heating the pan over the huge Wolf stove while Anatole organized eggs, milk, and flour for the batter. And I lamented, not for the first time, how little I knew about Bennett. I mean, I knew the big things, but not the details. Like, how could I not know what his favorite food was?

Anatole spooned batter into the cast-iron skillet, and after a moment he expertly flipped it and added a layer of Nutella. He started to added a capful of Cointreau, but I stopped him.

Not that, I said. *He doesn't need anything more like that.*

Anatole nodded, then scooped the crepe onto a plate

and folded it into quarters. It had a sweet aroma that I hoped would entice Bennett to eat.

I thanked them and took the plate upstairs to find Bennett pacing in his attic room, tapping some indecipherable rhythm on his thigh as he walked. I checked for earbuds, but he was tapping to some random beat in his head.

"Let's go," he said, when he saw me. "You and me, right now." He laid his hands on my shoulders. "We don't need anyone else. We can find his ashes together. End this all. We can do it."

"Bennett, I can't do *anything* with you this close—you smell like Asarum." It was a sickly sweet, almost rotten, gingery odor. I ducked from under his arms, ignoring the hurt look on his face. "Let's stick with the plan. I'll use the ring to search. You guard me. Okay?"

"I don't know," he said, shaking his head, confused and exhausted. "I don't know, Emma, what to do. I thought—if I could be with you, everything would be all right. But it's not, is it?"

I'd never seen him so unsure. He was normally so self-confident it came off as arrogance, unless you knew him. Knew how much he would do for the ones he loved. Like me.

I grabbed his hand, and he tried to pull away. "We'll talk about it tomorrow. Just stay with me now. Let me take care of you. I brought you something to eat. Anatole said it was one of your favorites."

He stared at the plate. "Crepes. Those are my favorite." He sounded like he was no longer sure. He took a bite, then set the fork down. "I'll finish it later," he said, which we both knew was a lie.

"Bennett, you have to eat," I said.

"I need to rest first. Can I hold you?" he asked. "Would that be okay?"

"Yeah," I said, even though I didn't really want to be held. Not with that whirlpool of power swirling around him. He lay with his back against the headboard and I settled in the crook of his arm. He squeezed me for a moment, then closed his eyes.

"Is it true, what Harry said?" he asked, his eyes still closed. "That you're always crying about me."

"Not always."

"He's a good friend, standing up to me like that. You bring out the best in people."

Not in you, I thought.

And as if he could read my mind, he said, "Even in me."

His breathing began to even out as he fell asleep. But as I lay there against his bony frame, trying to ignore the unhealthy power burning through him, tears streamed down my cheeks. This wasn't how it was supposed to be. Love shouldn't make you miserable. You should feel at home in your boyfriend's arms, sheltered and safe, not worried and guilty.

This was all my fault, and there was only one thing I could do about it. And it wouldn't make either of us any happier.

. . .

I dozed for a time, and when I woke I found Bennett standing at the window, staring into the darkness. He looked lean and dangerous—like a stranger.

I watched him for a minute before I spoke. "You've taken this whole bad-boy thing too far."

He stiffened. "Is that what you think this is? An act?" He turned toward me. "I love you, Emma, and I'm doing this—"

"No! Don't say it. You're not doing this for me. You're not killing yourself for *me*."

"I'm doing this to kill Neos. To help you kill him. I'm doing this for my sister and my parents, for Martha, Yoshiro, and the others. And yeah, maybe I'm doing this for myself, because you're not the only one with a destiny."

Something about his tone stopped me for a moment. "You . . . Simon thinks *we* have a secret. But it's you, isn't it? What's your secret, Bennett?"

"I can't tell you," he said, his eyes downcast.

"You swore to always tell me the truth."

"I'm not going to lie. I'm just not going to tell you."

I choked back tears as the truth hit me. "You think you're going to die."

"We're fighting Neos," he said, his blue eyes cold. "Any of us might die."

"No. No, you're *planning* on—" I swallowed. "I can't even say it. I won't forgive you, Bennett. If you leave me, I will not forgive you."

"I'm learning, Emma." His blue eyes brightened.

"I've learned to use the Asarum to absorb power, I can use it to—"

"No!" I snapped. "Stop taking the Asarum, or . . . I can't see you like this."

The words hung in the air almost like his power, sickening and impossible to ignore.

"So this is it?" he said, after a long moment. "You're done waiting for me?"

"I'm not done waiting for you, Bennett. I'll never be done. But this isn't you."

I expected anger and disappointment. What I didn't anticipate was his picking up the antique wooden chair and smashing it against the wall until it shattered. Then he hurled the standing mirror across the room and flung his bookshelf to the floor, and probably would've totaled the room if his parents hadn't raced inside the attic, drawn by the noise.

"What is going on here?" Mr. Stern asked.

"We're breaking up," Bennett said. "You should be happy."

A look crossed between his parents that I couldn't even begin to discern. Mostly because I couldn't handle my own emotions. This is what I wanted, right? If we weren't together, he could stop taking the Asarum. That's all that mattered, I told myself, as Bennett shoved past them and down the rickety stairs.

"Are you okay?" Mrs. Stern asked me.

I nodded. I hadn't been afraid that he'd hurt me—he never would—but the mirror shattering had made a sickening noise, and his anger was so raw and out of control. I'd only ever seen him this furious around wraiths. And it was hard not to feel superstitious about the mirror. We really didn't need more bad luck.

"That was my great-grandfather's chair," Mr. Stern said mournfully.

"Honestly, John, I don't think broken furniture is our biggest problem," Mrs. Stern said, but I felt her summoning Celeste, who appeared instantly with a broom and dustpan.

Celeste flashed a me a wide-eyed look of surprise and empathy before kneeling to clean the mess. Splintered wood and shards of glass were scattered over the attic floor.

When Mrs. Stern tried to comfort me, I told her I needed time alone. As they left, I stood at the attic window, watching Bennett's Land Rover peel out over the gravel drive. My heart thumped inside me, feeling like it was going to burst from my chest.

Then I noticed a metal canister on the bedside table beside my phone. It was a box of loose-leaf chai tea, from a fancy tea shop in Manhattan. And when I scrolled through my phone, I saw that Bennett had added ten more apps and a playlist of twenty new songs. Instead of being happy, I only felt worse.

I didn't go to school the next day. Simon never would've let me get away with that, but the Sterns either didn't care or were stuck in the mire of their own depression. How would I know? I never even left my room.

Natalie and Lukas both knocked. I'd learned my lesson, though, and shoved my chair under the handle so Natalie couldn't barge in. I heard her trying to talk Lukas into smashing in, but he refused. Either he didn't want to get in trouble with the Sterns, or he understood I just wanted to be alone. It was more of a guy reaction to a problem. I'd noticed girls often liked to cry and relive every moment of distress with a friend. I wasn't that kind of girl.

Instead, I listened to Bennett's songs over and over. I kept my laptop in bed with me so I could look up the lyrics online and memorize them. One of the songs was about how life had no music "before you." That's how I felt, like all the music and color had gone out of the world. Sometimes a song could really hit you, even if it was from an artist who usually sang about her lady parts.

But I also wasn't the kind of girl who was destroyed by a breakup, so the next morning I got dressed and went looking for Mrs. Stern.

She wasn't having coffee in the breakfast nook, so I grabbed a cup of tea and went to find her in her office. The room was elegant and feminine, with botanical prints displayed along the beige walls, delicate shelves holding books and a seashell collection, and a large white desk in the center of the room. Mrs. Stern sat behind it, tapping on her laptop. She glanced up over her navy blue reading glasses when she heard me enter.

Maybe it was the glasses, but she didn't appear her

usual polished self. There were circles under her eyes and her normally sleek ponytail frizzily escaped its rubber band.

"Have you heard from him?" I asked.

"No," she answered.

"I'm sorry about . . . everything."

"You've done nothing to apologize for."

"I need a written excuse," I said. "For missing school yesterday."

I half expected her to say, "Oh, you missed a day?" but instead she said, "I called and told them you were ill." She eyed my uniform. "Looks like I don't need to call again this morning?"

I shook my head and stood there a moment longer, waiting for I don't know what. Something about Bennett, I guess. How much we both worried and cared about him.

Instead, she said, "Lukas and I will guard you while you search the grounds tonight."

"Then shouldn't I stay home today and rest up?" I asked, hopefully.

"You rested enough yesterday," she said.

"Could you name all the parts of the eye?" a voice whispered into my ear.

I spun, my heart pounding—and saw a kid from AP Biology standing next to me. We were in the Lame Lounge, digging through our lockers after a test I'd been unprepared for.

"Huh?" I said. "What?"

"The eye," he repeated, his Adam's apple bobbing nervously. "I think I mixed up the sclera and ciliary body."

"Yeah," I admitted. "I got confused, too." I'd confused him with a ghost I imagined whispering in my ear.

Then again, a lot of things were confusing me. Like every time we looked at a diagram of an eyeball, I thought of the empty sockets of wraiths, as though someone had plucked out their eyes for a biology exam.

The bio kid had said something I missed, so I said, "Oh. Um, what?"

He ducked his head and scuttled away, like I'd brushed him off. I kept having conversations like that all day, my mind on ghosts—and on figuring out how I'd search the grounds tonight in my ghostly form.

I decided to start in the attic and make my way down through the school, checking all the places that weren't accessible to the living. But meanwhile, I'd keep searching. So at lunch, I checked a little-used classroom that Harry had suggested. "There's a closet in back that's so creepy I almost didn't drink there."

"Almost?" I'd said.

"Well, nobody ever bothered me," he'd explained. "So I just drank until I stopped noticing the stench of sulfur."

He'd been kidding about the sulfur, but not the creepiness. And when I stepped inside the closet, I found out why. It was haunted.

By a cat. Yeah, a dead cat. I'd never seen a ghost animal before.

Here, kitty, kitty, I said, making clicking noises with my tongue.

It jumped me. I screamed as it clawed its way up my chest. Like any ghost, it had the ability to burn me, and its claws dug through my uniform like hot needles jabbing my skin.

Without thinking, I grabbed hold of it. Big mistake. My hands started burning, and the ghost cat dug in even deeper until I unraveled it with a bolt of dispelling energy. I practically fell out of the closet, unbuttoning my shirt to check my wounds and finding little fiery marks along my ribs.

And that's how Harry found me. "Good lord, Vaile," he said. "Keep your shirt on."

"Ow, ow, it hurts," I said, not caring that he could see my bra.

Once he realized I wasn't kidding, he turned serious. "Do you need to go to the hospital again?" he asked, acting very gentlemanly about my exposed underwear.

"No, I'm fine. It was just a cat."

"Was it on fire?" he asked, perplexed.

"It was a ghost."

"A ghost cat," he said blankly.

"Ow. Yes, in the closet. It probably attacked you the whole time you were in there. You just couldn't feel it."

"Emma," he said, "I'd like to go on record as saying that your life is seriously messed up."

"I know." Then I started giggling. "Wait'll I tell Ben—" I stopped laughing. You don't call the guy you dumped to tell him you found a ghost cat in a closet.

"How is he?" Harry asked. "What happened after I left?"

"We broke up."

"Good."

"Not good." I exhaled. "Bennett needs me and I told him to go away. That I didn't want him like this. What kind of person does that?"

Harry stepped closer, concern etched in that odd, aristocratic face. "A good person. He's hurting and he's hooked, true. But the first step in recovery is—"

"If this conversation ends with 'namaste,' I'm going to hit you."

Harry smiled. "Then I'll say no more."

That was so unlike Harry, letting a subject drop because I was uncomfortable with it—usually he *lived* for those subjects—that I gave him a quick hug.

"What was that for?" he asked as the bell rang, ending lunch.

"After Coby died, I didn't think I'd have another friend who cared like that, who I could trust. You're like him, only—"

"I know." He nodded solemnly. "Better-looking."

"Right," I said as we walked off together. The smile on my face felt good.

11

The bell rang a minute after I took my seat in World Lit. I'd called my mom on the walk over, but hadn't bothered leaving a message. I wasn't sure she even knew how to retrieve them. She and my dad considered themselves Luddites and used current technology as little as possible. They were the only ones who found this charming.

I faked my way through *Zorba the Greek*, and when class ended, I redialed her.

She picked up on the third ring. "Hello? Hello?" She'd never understood that cells took a second longer to engage than landlines.

"It's me, mom."

"Hello? Who is this?" Or that if you looked at your phone before answering, you could tell who was calling.

"Emma!" I practically yelled, over the commotion.

I was standing in the hallway, and a bunch of rowdy ski team boys were psyching themselves up for this afternoon's meet. You wouldn't think cross-country skiers would get so wild, but they were jumping up and batting at a banner for Parents' Night. Which was one more thing I needed to talk to my mom about.

I plugged the ear not attached to my phone and listened to my mother crabbing about not being able to hear me. "... and that boyfriend of yours is a mess. Simon's completely fed up with him, and I don't blame him."

"That's not why I called," I lied. Actually, I'd hoped she'd tell me that he was there, and okay. At least, as okay as he got these days. "But, um ... is he there right now?"

"What? No, he's not here. I thought he was with you. Wait, your father's talking. He says Bennett was here. But he's gone again. I'm not sure how he's supposed to be protecting you *or* Simon when he's—"

"Parents' Night is in a few weeks," I interrupted, as the ski boys started shouting some cross-country fight song. They took this way too seriously.

"What? I can barely hear you. Parents' Night?"

"Yeah, are you coming?"

"Do you need a permission slip?" she asked.

"It's *Parents'* Night!"

"Honestly, Emma," she said, a little exasperated, "I can't hear a word you're saying. Call us later. We love you."

"Love you, too."

I considered calling Simon, but needed to get to class, so I texted him on the way. *Pls help B. I beg u.*

. . .

I cut through the main hall on my way to Western Civ. The two-story room was always crowded between classes, and while enormous medieval tapestries hung on the wall, they did nothing to muffle the voices echoing off the marble floors and the sweeping stairway.

Halfway across, I saw Lukas chatting with a cute girl I didn't know, probably a senior. They were sitting on a couch across from the big stone hearth, half hidden by the huge centerpiece of silk flowers on the coffee table.

I said "hey" as I passed, hurrying to class, then saw Natalie stalking closer. I knew that look all too well—she was about to make a scene.

I called her name, but she ignored me and stomped toward Lukas. She gave the girl an evil look, then crawled into Lukas's lap and began kissing him. It was a bold move, even for Natalie, and Lukas wasn't into it. He stood, Natalie still in his arms, and set her down on her feet.

Her eyes narrowed, and I lost sight of them in the crowd. But then Sara stepped out from under the staircase, where she'd been talking to one of her parasophomours. "Bastard," she said.

"Whats-his-name?" I nodded at the parasophomour's retreating back.

"No, Lukas. How could he treat Natalie like that?"

I watched Sara's face. She was so pretty and rich and popular that I still never quite believed how *nice* she was. "I'll never understand you," I said.

"What? Why?"

"Because I know you like him. A normal person would be happy things weren't perfect between them." I remembered how she'd made me pretty for my first date with Coby. She could've sabotaged me, but she hadn't. "You never operate out of jealousy."

"Emma, look around. Thatcher is a hotbed of hot boys. What's there to be jealous about? It's high school—nobody hooks up forever."

That thought stayed with me the rest of the day. Was I a freak for thinking I'd love Bennett forever? Yeah, we'd broken up, but I still loved him. We weren't over, not even close. But was it our shared determination to kill Neos that kept us together? Would we still want each other if we survived the fight?

I couldn't help thinking Sara was right; we were so young. It was naive to think that Bennett was the only guy I'd ever love. And yet I did.

"Whoa, Kylee, where'd you learn *that*?"

Kylee was ninety pounds soaking wet, yet she regularly kicked my butt in fencing. I could *fight*, but I couldn't *fence*. It just didn't come naturally to me.

Today, for some reason, Kylee was fighting like me. She'd loosened her form and attacked aggressively, with the same brutal edge that the Rake had beaten into me. It wasn't like Kylee at all. She normally executed her thrusts with composed grace. This was sloppier, yet more powerful.

Even after she disarmed me, I suppressed the urge to respond in kind; I didn't want to hurt her. She was good, but I was better.

Kylee grunted as I retrieved my foil, not bothering to answer my question.

I got back into position. "En guard."

She came at me with a cross-cut. I blocked her, but didn't return the attack, waiting for Coach to realize that someone else was fighting dirty for once.

Coach didn't seem to notice, but the ghost jocks really enjoyed themselves. They shimmered into existence the moment Kylee disarmed me the first time, and my spine tingled even more than usual from their ghostly presence.

Cat fight, Moorehead said, from his perch in the bleachers. *Bet you Emma gets knocked on her butt.*

How much? Craven asked. He was lying backward on the bench, his head lower than his feet, examining me upside down.

Ten minutes alone in the girls' locker, Moorehead answered.

Done!

Yeesh. Somehow it hadn't occurred to me that they were haunting the girls' locker room. I scowled at them as I deflected a fleché. *Why don't you bet about whether I'm going to compel you to flip off the bleachers and land on* your *butts?*

They were unimpressed, even though they knew I could do it. I fended off Kylee's renewed attack, retreating across the mat, and waited for a return insult.

Instead, Craven said, *Something's wrong.*

The two of them drifted through the bleachers and landed on the floor of the gym. *There's another ghost here,* Moorehead said, serious for once. *Maybe a wraith. One of his.*

Neos. I dropped my guard slightly as I summoned my power, and Kylee shed all pretence of fencing and came at me in a vicious assault. I deflected one attack after another as Kylee chuckled. Only . . . the chuckle sounded like a man. And it hadn't come from Kylee's mouth. Her face was covered with a mask, but the laugh had definitely been male. She was possessed.

I switched my grip on my foil and summoned my power. *There's only one way this can end,* I told the ghost inside her.

Yes, he said. *But you don't know what it is.*

Leave her!

I only obey Neos. Kylee slashed at me and I let the blow land—a stinging pain like a whip—and caught her wrist.

You'll obey me, I snarled, and compelled the ghost from her body like shucking a slug off a stem.

Kylee fainted to the mat and a ghost stood in her place, tall and muscular and hard-faced. *I came for the ring around your neck.*

Tell Neos to buy his own jewelry, I said, shooting him with dispelling energy flashing from my fingertips.

The ghost didn't flinch. *Neos will reward me in*—he started, then faded into an oil slick on the gym floor.

For a moment, it felt like the whole world was silent.

"Emma!" Coach shouted, running toward us. "What did you do to Kylee?"

"I—I—"

"She fainted," Natalie called from across the room. "I was watching. Kylee just fainted."

Coach eyed me suspiciously as Kylee started rousing, then sent one of the girls for the nurse and told me she considered this my fault. I was irresponsible and inconsiderate. I didn't have the style for fencing, and I didn't have the sense not to bully poor little Kylee. She told me to expect an "incomplete" as my grade, because she wouldn't let me fence again this year. Then she sent me to the locker room to change.

I shuffled out of the gym, worrying about Kylee, and who Neos would send next to retrieve my ring. I felt a ghostly tinge nearby and wanted to lash out at Craven and Moorehead, but didn't have the energy.

I sat on a bench staring at my locker, and a couple of girls I didn't recognize came in for the next class. I ignored them, lost in my own sulky thoughts, and suddenly the world tilted and I wasn't looking at the locker anymore.

I was looking at the underside of the bench.

Lying on my back on the floor, my head throbbing in pain, a puddle of water soaking through my shirt.

Above me, a girl said, "Oh, did she fall?" But there was a ghostly echo in my mind—I heard a ghost speaking at the same time: *Grab the ring.*

A fist closed on my hair and yanked my head, and another hand grabbed my necklace and pulled. The chain snapped. My ring—Emma's ring—rolled across the tile floor. One of the girls, who I now knew were possessed, snatched it, and spoke to the other. *Does Neos want her dead? Or does he have other plans for her?*

He wants the ring to help him claim her. Now that he has the ring, he'll—

Then I heard a new voice. *Hey, girls, you looking for the showers?* Craven asked.

The sound of fighting and swearing echoed in the locker room as I faded away.

When I returned to consciousness, I was still on the floor, still looking at the bottom of the bench. Except now Craven was sitting there, his face even paler than usual.

I moaned and sat up. "What happened?"

Isn't it obvious? They bashed you on the head and stole your ring. Craven looked toward the corner. *We fought them off, but he's hurt pretty bad.*

I followed his gaze to the corner, where Moorehead was curled in a ball, slowly unraveling.

He's . . . he's fading, Craven said. *I'm going to be alone.* For once, his tone wasn't filled with sarcasm. He was really worried.

I stood unsteadily, then almost fell as pain burst in my head and my knees wobbled. I dropped beside Moorehead and said, *Do you want to stay?*

I do, Moorehead told me feebly. *But I can't.*

I blinked away tears of pain, willing myself to not think about losing the ring—not yet. Instead, I focused on trying to save Moorehead. I thought if I could summon him, maybe it would lodge his ghost more solidly in this world. My stomach churned as summoning power surged through me. The blow to my head was still making me woozy, and I couldn't get a grip on Moorehead. Instead of helping him, he seemed to be fading further.

I'm sorry. I don't know what to do. I can't— And then it hit me. What about the principle of reflexivity Simon had been talking about? Could I use my dispelling power to heal Moorehead?

I glanced at Moorehead. *Okay. I'm not sure this is going to work.* But it was better than doing nothing, than watching him fade into nothing. I gathered a line of dispelling energy, then twisted it in my mind, so that instead of hurting him, it would heal. If this didn't work, I was out of options, so despite feeling like I might pass out again, I poured power into him. For a moment, nothing happened. Then he grew firmer, more coherent, his spectral self reknitting.

"It worked!" I said aloud. Simon had been right. All our powers worked in both directions.

Craven slumped in relief. *Much better. We owe you.*

You fought those ghosts for me.

Because this is the girls' locker room, Moorehead explained, gesturing widely. *The inner sanctum.*

The holy of holies, Craven intoned. *We don't let just* anyone *in here. Besides, we couldn't stop them. We tried to keep them from getting your ring, but they were too strong.*

Still, I told them, *you tried. And you probably saved my life.*

Well, you saved his death, Craven said.

I tried to smile, but couldn't manage more than a pained grin. Not only because my head hurt, but I'd lost the ring. Neos had wanted one thing, and now he had it.

"The possessed girls hit you with a field hockey stick?" Mrs. Stern asked. "Did you see the nurse?"

It was an hour after school, and I was sitting around the breakfast nook with Mrs. Stern, Lukas, and Natalie. Mr. Stern paced the floor, occasionally stepping through Anatole or Celeste, who kept the table stocked with tea and cookies.

I'd just told them what happened at fencing class, that Neos had used the ghost possessing Kylee to manipulate me into the locker room alone; then the other possessed girls had attacked, and I'd lost the ring.

"I made her go to the nurse," Natalie answered. "She said Emma's okay."

"I am," I said, rubbing my head. "No concussion, just a goose egg."

"Coach thought she was faking, for attention."

"Coach hates me."

"I'll have a word with her," Mr. Stern said, a hint of his son's protectiveness in his eyes.

"That's hardly the issue," Mrs. Stern said. "We've lost

the ring. So not only does Neos have this new advantage over us, but Emma can't search Thatcher for his ashes as a ghost."

"Are we even sure why he wanted the ring?" Lukas asked.

I fiddled with the sugar cookie on my plate. "I think I'm part of his plan. The ghosts said something about him claiming me."

"He intends to possess you," Mrs. Stern said. "To use the body of the most powerful ghostkeeper as his own. We suspected that much already."

I thought about the snaky ghost visions again. What if he'd already started, and the visions were part of that? It made me wonder if I could trust myself.

"We can still search the school," Natalie said. "Just not with Emma as a ghost."

"So far, everything we've done has played into Neos's hands." Mrs. Stern paused to sip her tea. "For once I'd like to be a step ahead of him."

Mr. Stern stopped pacing. "And Simon expects him to attack soon."

"Natalie, did you feel the ghosts at school today, in your fencing class?" Mrs. Stern asked. "Why didn't you help Emma?"

Natalie looked stricken. "Me?"

"You *are* a ghostkeeper."

"Okay." I set my half-eaten cookie aside. "She gets the point. Stop picking on her."

"I'm not picking on her, Emma. I'm trying to assess our strength. How much weaker are you?" she asked Natalie. "Since you and Lukas started . . . seeing each other?"

"I'm not sure. A little?" Natalie said, miserably. I noticed she didn't look at Lukas.

"This isn't her fault," I said. "I'm the one who let them take the ring." I downed the rest of my tea. "The only thing that matters is finding those ashes. Without them, we've got nothing."

Despite being in an ongoing battle with Neos, I still had school and homework. It would be nice if I could claim a ghost ate my homework, but I doubt un-cute Mr. Jones would believe me. So after dinner, I spent a couple hours catching up and finished my *Zorba* paper. Then I knocked on Natalie's bedroom door. She didn't answer. I knew Lukas was downstairs eating his second dinner, so I pushed open the door, presuming I wasn't interrupting anything.

Natalie was buried under the covers, her laptop open beside her. "Go away."

"No." I sat beside her. "I know you want to talk."

"I do not," she said.

"Yes, you do. I can tell."

"You're interfering with my celebrity gossip. How am I supposed to survive without knowing what they're wearing to the Golden Globes?"

I was momentarily distracted by the photos on her

screen. "Wouldn't it be awesome to have an excuse to dress up like that?"

"There's prom next year," she said.

"Yeah, I guess." Though I had no idea where I'd be going to school next year, or if I'd even want to go to prom. I stared at her until she flipped her computer closed.

"Fine," she said.

"What's going on with you and Lukas?"

"You mean today in the main hall?"

"No, I mean the whole thing. You and Lukas together. You haven't told me anything."

She licked her lips. "I know. I didn't know what to say to you. I thought you'd disapprove. I'm scared. That's what's going on."

"Because you like him more than he likes you?"

"Oh, he likes me," she said, sounding like herself again. "He definitely likes me."

"Then what are you afraid of? Losing your powers?"

She didn't answer for a moment, then said, "Ever since that last battle with Neos, with all those ghasts and wraiths, the siren trying to drown me, I've—I kind of lost my nerve. You don't know what it's like; you're Emma Vaile, Warrior Queen of the Dear Departed. You think I'm all brave, but I'm not."

"You're scared of ghosts?" I was astounded. This was like my ex–best friend Abby all over again. "You don't want to see them anymore?"

"What? No, you bonehead, I'm not afraid of ghosts, I'm afraid of *dying*. I don't want Neos to kill me. Or you.

Or any of us. How would you feel, if you couldn't protect yourself?"

"Terrified."

"What if you couldn't protect *me*?"

I didn't say anything. If I didn't think I could protect her and Lukas, I'd freeze completely.

"Yeah," she said. "I'm a summoner. We're the opposite of badass. And now that I finally learned how to banish, my powers are fading. Lukas is taking my power. And he's . . ."

"What is he?"

"Well, he's totally fantastic, you know that." She bit her lower lip. "And you know how he *looks* like he knows how to kiss and stuff?"

"Yeah?"

"Well, he does." She blew a puff of air. "Believe me, he totally knows. He—"

"Okay, okay! Yuck. He's like a brother to me."

"Well, he's like a hot boyfriend to me. And I really like him. But he's getting stronger."

"And you're getting weaker."

She nodded morosely. "If we don't stop, I'm going to lose my powers completely."

"Is that such a bad thing?" I asked, biting my lip. "You sound like you don't know anymore."

"Maybe not," she said, "but am I the girl who gives up everything to be with a guy?"

"No."

"*Hell* no. And do you really think you can do this without my lame-ass help?"

"Yes. I can do this without you." I didn't want to guilt her into this.

She lifted an eyebrow.

"Okay," I said. "Fine. I need you, Natalie. I know I have more power, but you *are* braver. I *can't* do it without you."

She flipped her long dark hair to one shoulder and began to braid it while she thought. When she got to the bottom, she ripped it apart and started again. When she ran out of hair the second time, she said, "I'm going to break up with him."

"You don't—why can't you—" I stopped, because I couldn't think of another solution. She had to break up with him or she'd lose her powers completely.

"It's okay," she said. "I like him. A lot. But it's not like we're destined to be together through the centuries—or apart—or whatever you and Bennett have going on."

"Are you sure?" At the moment, I wasn't sure what Bennett and I had going on. Despite being broken up, I knew it wasn't over. It was hard to believe it ever would be.

"Yeah, I'm sure. We're not even in the same league of eternally-together-and-forever-screwed as you two. It's just—"

Lukas burst into the room without bothering to knock, which made me wonder how often they were in here "getting all dirty," as Natalie liked to say.

"Oh." He looked surprised to see me. "Hey, Emma."

"I was just going," I said.

"No, wait," Natalie told me. Then she turned to Lukas and said, "Dude, it's over."

Yikes. She couldn't wait for me to leave the room? I stared at the carpet and tried to make myself invisible.

"What's over?" he asked, clearly confused.

"Us, you idiot," Natalie said. "Emma needs me."

His face fell. "What if I don't want it to be over?"

"You don't?" she said in a small voice.

I came out from my invisibility shield long enough to say, "Lukas, she's losing her abilities. You stay together any longer and she won't even *see* ghosts anymore. You'll have taken all her power."

Lukas stared at Natalie, shock on his face. "Is it really that bad?"

"Yeah."

"Why didn't you tell me?" He looked horror-stricken.

"Because I was afraid. Scared of fighting ghosts, and scared of—" She shrugged. "Of losing you."

He rubbed his eyes. "This sucks. It's not fair. I mean, my parents . . . But you, you're the—you and me, we're just totally . . ."

Natalie nodded, tears escaping her eyes. "We totally are."

"You mean were." Lukas swore and smacked the wall. He didn't say anything, but I'm pretty sure he was also about to cry. He turned and stalked into the hallway before we could see him breaking down.

Natalie was shaking, and I cradled her as I wiped tears from her face. "I'm so sorry. I didn't want this to happen."

She sniffled. "I should be thanking you."

"For encouraging you to break up with Lukas? You should be cursing me."

"Not for that. For needing me. For not letting me throw it all away. Ghostkeeping is the one thing that makes me special. Lukas is great, and I guess I kind of love him. But he's not the only guy out there. There'll be other boys. And one day, even men." She flashed me a watery smile. "I'm just getting started."

"It's not the ghostkeeping that makes you special, Natalie. It's you."

The next few days dragged past. Natalie and Lukas had awful, stilted conversations in the breakfast nook, and were overly polite when they met in the hall. And they were so obviously unhappy and uncomfortable that the whole house turned gloomy.

I wasn't any better. I felt like a failure for losing the ring, and like a bad friend for my part in the breakup. Plus I was racked with worry and guilt for telling Bennett I couldn't see him when he was hurting so badly. And I knew that the Sterns were struggling with their own anxieties.

But worse than the tension was the sense of dread. Neos had won. He'd stolen the ring and was gathering his armies, waiting for the perfect time to strike. Holding off until he *knew* he'd win. And all we could do was wait and worry and hope for the best—and, of course, search for the ashes.

Max and Edmund worked their way through the

library's collections, and Coby flitted through Thatcher's walls whenever he wasn't busy spying in the Beyond. Lukas and Natalie searched during every class break and after school every day—though not together anymore. And I dug around with Harry and Sara, who between them knew every nook and cranny of the school.

We found old sports trophies, mounds of ashes from secret smokers, bizarre pottery projects from the '70s, zinc and magnesium powder in the science class cabinets, containers of dubious herbs in the cafeteria, and containers of high-grade herb in a few student lockers.

But not Neos's ashes.

Before lunch one day, I flopped into a chair in the Lame Lounge and slipped my aching feet from my boots. We were doing everything we could, and it still wasn't enough. I didn't know what else we could try, though.

"Hey," a voice said.

I looked up and saw Kylee. She'd been absent from school for a week, hit much harder than Britta, who'd felt better hours after her possession, despite all the violence. That was Britta for you.

"Hey!" I said, standing to hug her. "Feeling better?"

"Mostly," she said hesitantly.

"You look better," I said, even though she didn't, not really. She was even paler and skinnier than usual. "You know what you need? Chicken soup. I'll have my—" My what—ghost chef? "I'll bring you some tomorrow."

"Oh, no, thanks." She bit her thumbnail. "I just—wanted to say I'm sorry."

"For what?"

"For getting you in trouble with Coach. And I don't really remember, but I . . ." She shifted uncomfortably. "I feel like I sort of attacked you."

I tried a reassuring smile. "Well, we were fencing! That was the whole point."

She grabbed my arm, suddenly urgent. "Emma, it was like someone was inside of me, like I wasn't in control. My parents think I've been doing drugs, but I swear I haven't."

"I know you haven't," I said. "You're going to be fine."

"I think I'm going crazy," she blurted, her eyes scared.

"Kylee, look at me. You are not going crazy. I promise. Okay?"

She nodded doubtfully.

"I *promise.* Kylee, you're half my size and you kick my ass in fencing every day. You're *tough*. Believe me, you'll feel better."

She said "Okay," but the fear remained in her eyes as she headed to class. More than fear: like being possessed had made her mistrust herself. I could relate.

After she left, I found myself shaking with anger. A white-hot fury, fueled by all my dread and guilt, my grief for the dead, and now seeing little Kylee with that broken look in her eyes. My sense of futility and failure all came together in my mind. And I took those feelings and clenched them like a fist of power, and sent a burst of words into the Beyond: *I'm going to find you, Neos. And I'm going to make you pay.*

I hoped my message would find him, the way I'd

found Rachel. I didn't know what it would accomplish, but it made me less afraid. And I felt more like we still had a chance.

The bell sounded, but I remained in my chair, lost in thought through most of the next period. Then I rummaged in my bag for my phone and clicked through to Bennett's number. It rang five times before I got his voice mail, and I wondered if he was sitting on the other end of the line, waiting for me to leave a message.

"It's me," I said. "I wanted to make sure you're okay. And . . . well, there were a few more possessions at school. I guess Simon told you. I lost the ring. And I lost . . ." I wanted to say "you," but couldn't. "We can't find the ashes, and we're just waiting for the other shoe to drop, for Neos to make the next move. I don't know what to do. I miss you."

I hung up, before he could hear me sniffle. Then I began to cry, because the truth was, no matter how furious I got, the fight had gone out of me. I couldn't deal anymore. I hadn't been able to protect Kylee, I couldn't help Natalie and Lukas, I couldn't help Bennett, or guard the ring, or find the ashes. How was I supposed to keep the whole school safe?

There was a twitch in the atmosphere, and I turned to find Coby standing beside me. *Emma, what happened? I heard what you sent into the Beyond about making Neos pay—* everyone *heard it. Are you okay?*

Yeah. I took a deep breath and dried my eyes. *I'm fine.*

Just crying from happiness again?

I almost smiled. *I'm tired. That's all.*

I can't imagine why—you're only supposed to do everything around here. Dispel ghosts, help your friends, find the ashes, figure out what your aunt Rachel is doing, protect your classmates. Oh, and kill Neos.

Do I sound like that? I asked, appalled. *God, I really am an emo whiner.*

He laughed, which always made me happy. *At least I've got Harry and Sara covered. You can cross them off your list.*

You've been guarding them?

He nodded. *Whenever I'm not poking around the Beyond. You can't be with them all the time.*

They need full-time protection. You didn't see what Britta did to them. We can put the ghost jocks on them, I suggested. *That way you can stay longer in the Beyond and warn us when Neos is on his way.*

Coby frowned. *They'll make rude comments about Sara.*

Better than her getting possessed. And she won't hear anyway. I hate to ask you, but if we don't learn what Neos is doing with my ring and his ashes, we're totally screwed.

Okay. I've been keeping my distance from Neos, but I'll get closer.

But stay safe, I begged.

He eyed me thoughtfully. *It's that ass Bennett making you unhappy, isn't it?*

No, I said, and when he gave me a look, *Okay, a little.*

I wouldn't have made you unhappy, he said as he faded away.

"No," I said aloud. "You wouldn't have."

My stomach rumbled as the fourth period bell rang, and I grabbed my lunch out of my locker and went to join Natalie, Harry, and Sara at our usual table in the cafeteria. Lukas came in a moment later, looking unsure where to sit. I felt Natalie tense beside me, but she waved him over. She picked at the salad Anatole had packed her, and Lukas watched her for a moment before unpacking his sandwich. I ached for both of them. They couldn't be together, but they couldn't be apart, either.

Sara asked about Kylee, so I filled them in. "So she's back," I finished, "but she's kinda . . ."

"Haunted?" Harry asked.

I almost snapped at him for joking about it, then realized he was serious. "Yeah. Like she's lost something. And she looks like crap."

"Do you think she'll get better?" Natalie asked.

"I don't know." I looked around the room and found Britta sitting at a table with her friends, whispering and texting furiously.

"Britta looks all right," Harry said, echoing my thoughts.

"Yeah, figures that she'd . . ." I stopped, suddenly hearing a strange hissing sound over the regular lunchroom chatter.

Whispering. A dozen kids whispering to each other, all at once. Then more than a dozen—and pretty soon all conversation in the cafeteria had died away, and was replaced by wordless whispering.

"Well, *that's* not right," Harry said.

"Are they all looking at us?" Sara asked. "They're all looking at us."

"It's like a naked-at-school dream," Lukas said.

"I love that dream," Harry said.

We all gaped at him for a moment, despite the eerie whispering filling the room—then someone screamed. The sharp, high-pitched sound cut through the whispers and set my heart racing. Natalie and I exchanged a glance, and Lukas pushed his lunch aside, preparing for the worst.

"Who screamed?" I asked, my voice soft. "Where did it come from?"

"I don't know," Natalie said.

"Okay, if—" I didn't get any further, because the kids at the other tables abruptly rose from their seats. Chairs scraped the floor, and a sudden hush fell. They all stood with blank expressions on their faces, looking almost militaristic in their school uniforms.

"Crap," I said under my breath. "Crap, crap."

I summoned my power, and felt Natalie and Lukas doing the same. I sent tendrils through the room, searching for ghosts, prepared to compel them from kids' bodies . . . and felt nothing. If they were normal ghosts I would've sensed them immediately. But there was something about them possessing bodies that shielded them from me.

"Emma, what's happening?" Natalie asked, panic in her voice. "I can't feel a thing."

"Oh, God," Harry said. "I can't die yet—I haven't finished the ten steps."

I glanced at Lukas and he shook his head. "I've got nothing."

At some signal I didn't catch, the kids all turned in unison. They filed across the room in a martial line. As they neared our table, they swiveled their heads to stare at me.

"What are we going to do?" Sara cried. "There's too many of them."

"Get down, both of you," I told her and Harry. "Under the table."

"No," Sara said, holding her salad fork like a dagger.

"They're still human on the outside," Harry said, clenching his fists.

No time to argue. I raised my hands and sent invisible compelling energy throughout the room, not caring how I looked. But I found nothing. As the other kids marched from the room in a martial line, I couldn't compel a single ghost from anyone's body.

Then Britta, the last in line, paused at our table. "What are you, a scarecrow?" She flipped her hair toward me and said triumphantly, "Told you I'd get even!"

Harry was the first to get it. He started to laugh. Then it dawned on me. This wasn't Neos. I couldn't compel any ghosts, because they weren't possessed. This was Thatcher's version of a flash mob.

I began to giggle, and so did the others. I was so relieved we hadn't just witnessed the entire school being possessed, I was giddy. And for the first time ever, I sort of liked Britta.

"You got me," I said.

13

I couldn't sleep as I curled into bed that night. I played games on my phone and surfed the net for a while, but nothing worked. I needed to let off steam. So I kicked my covers to the end of the bed and traded my pj's for black leggings and my gray sweater, then went downstairs to Mr. Stern's study.

I hadn't visited the Rake for weeks. I clenched my fist in anticipation of sparring with him, a vicious, no-holds-barred brawl. But when I stepped into Mr. Stern's office, I found him sitting behind his desk, a small table lamp barely illuminating him.

"Has something happened, Emma?" Mr. Stern asked with genuine concern. "Another possession?"

"No, no. Everything's okay."

"For once," he said, relaxing in his chair, and I saw the empty tumbler on the desk next to him. He wasn't drunk, but I wondered about him, sitting here alone in the low-lit room, probably worrying about Bennett. "Can't sleep?"

I eyed the swords on the wall. "I thought I might practice."

"With those?"

"Yeah, I've been borrowing them. I hope that's okay."

Mr. Stern chuckled. "Of course. You know one of them belonged to your ancestor? Mine, too."

"I know." The first time I'd held one of the swords I'd had a major flashback to Emma's sparring with the Rake. I'd felt every nuance of her love for him. And when Bennett had taken the other sword, we had flashed back together. It had been one of the best moments of my life. I felt myself flush at the thought of it.

"Of course you do," Bennett's dad said. He gave me one of those stern looks he and his son were so famous for, then he unexpectedly grinned. "I went to Thatcher, too, young lady. Care to show me what you've got?"

"Um . . ." My eyes widened. Sparring with Bennett's dad in the ballroom? There was no way this would end well.

"C'mon, I promise not to hurt you." He held Emma's sword out to me.

I sort of freaked at the idea of flashing back with Bennett's dad. That was the only way this could get any worse.

"Can I have the other one?" I asked. "The one that didn't belong to Emma. I don't want a flashback."

"Flashback? I know you're a reader, but what—you also relive her memories?"

I nodded. "Her thoughts, her emotions. It's a little . . ."

"Disconcerting, I imagine."

"Yeah."

He handed me the other sword, and I followed him into the ballroom. I stood awkwardly as he whipped the sword back and forth, trying to get a feel for the rhythm.

"You're not going to warm up?" he asked.

"No, the . . . my trainer doesn't believe in warming up," I said, wondering why the Rake didn't appear. Was he lingering just over the threshold of the Beyond, waiting for Bennett's dad to leave? Why did he never show himself to his ancestors? Was he ashamed of the murders he'd committed to avenge Emma's death?

Or was he pulling away from me?

I forgot about the Rake, though, as Mr. Stern and I engaged. He was tall and strong, and I felt him holding back. We weren't in class at Thatcher, so I didn't feel confined to the rules, but I held back, too, moving a little less hesitantly to try to disarm him.

"Oho," Mr. Stern said, good humored, deftly defending himself.

I grinned and choreographed a second attack, discovering we were evenly matched as long as I didn't employ any of the dirty tricks the Rake taught me. We fought back and forth along the length of the room, blades clashing in unsurprising but vigorous moves.

There was no danger, like when I was practicing with the Rake, who'd trained me to kill. Instead it was pure, exhilarating fun, and opened up a side of Mr. Stern I hadn't seen before—lighthearted and funny.

Then he stepped back. "Very good. Now show me what you can *really* do."

I cocked my head. "Are you sure?"

"To me, you're an ordinary seventeen-year-old girl," Mr. Stern explained. "I can't sense ghosts anymore, so I can't sense your powers, either. Show me the extraordinary side of you, Emma."

He attacked again, without warning, and something in his face reminded me of Bennett and of the Rake. I deflected his blow, tossed the rapier into my left hand, and lunged for him. He scrambled backward in surprise, then slashed at me as I slipped beside him, hooking my foot around the back of his leg. He dropped to his knees and I stopped with the point of my blade an inch from his ear.

He knelt there silently for a moment, then laughed. "Three seconds! My God, Emma, well done."

"Thanks. I had an excellent teacher." I gave him a hand up and we flopped into the white upholstered easy chairs at the end of the room.

"And exactly who was that?" Mr. Stern asked.

That's when the Rake chose to shimmer into existence. He was rather dramatic about it, somehow adding a little glow to his appearance. Normally, he just looked like a regular person, if dashing and dissolute—and somewhat pale.

Mr. Stern looked dumbfounded. "Is that . . . ? I shouldn't be able to see him."

"The first Bennett Stern." Well, at least that we knew of. I was pretty sure there was another one who lived back with the Emma in the tapestry at the Knell. "How can you see him?"

"I don't know. But it happened once before," he said,

"at Bennett's naming ceremony, which we held in this room."

Has it never occurred to you that ghosts really do haunt? the Rake asked sardonically. *We can make ourselves appear to people, not only ghostkeepers. It just takes some effort.*

Is that why you're glowing in that odd way?

He lifted an eyebrow. *You say odd, I say charming.*

I smiled. *You're cocky tonight, aren't you?*

It pleases me to see you happy.

You've been avoiding me, I accused him.

He shrugged. *You don't need me as much as you once did.*

"Why is he here?" Mr. Stern asked. He could see him, but of course couldn't communicate with him. "Why did he come?"

To see you, the Rake told me.

I shrugged. "I think I remind him of his Emma."

Less and less, the Rake said. *You are growing into yourself.*

Is that why you've been missing? You don't see her in me anymore?

The Rake ignored me, stalking toward the window to inspect the darkness.

"This isn't the first time, is it?" Mr. Stern realized. "That's why you fight so well. He taught you."

I nodded. "Yeah, he even fought with me. The day Neos came to kill Martha. He's been like . . . a hero," I finished, wanting the Rake to know how grateful I was to him.

Mr. Stern inspected me. "You're quite dear to those who care for you, aren't you? Martha, the ghosts, your friends." He seemed to struggle with some emotion for a moment. "My son. I can see why he fell in love with you."

How could he not? The Rake turned back from the windows. *It's destiny.*

"Thank you," I told Mr. Stern.

I wanted to believe the Rake about me and Bennett; but then again, destiny wasn't always a good thing.

"Is it me, or is this semester a lot harder?" I asked Sara on the way out of Trig the next day. I was beginning to think my teachers had gone easy on me last semester, because I'd transferred in late. Or maybe I just couldn't deal with everything else that was going on.

"It's easier if you're doing homework instead of searching for undead remains," Sara said, as we wandered the crowded hall together. "Thatcher's notoriously hard-core. Looks good on college applications, though, even if you get Bs."

"What about Cs?"

"Cs, not so much."

I bit my lip. "Will you study for the Trig test with me?" I was even falling behind in one of my best subjects.

"Sure," she said. "Chais and cramming at my house?"

"Sounds good. I've got some great chai Bennett brought—" I stopped, because the thought of Bennett hurt. "Anyway."

"You still haven't told me what happened," she said.

I opened my mouth to explain, but caught sight of

Max, waving a pizza and a liter of Coke at me from the end of the hall. I was getting an incomplete in fencing anyway, so I'd been using the period to search more. No reason I couldn't do it while eating pizza. "I better go see what Max wants."

Sara gave him a look. "Does he seriously think those pants work for him?" she teased, before she headed down the stairs that led to the girls' locker room.

"She likes me, doesn't she?" Max said, when I caught up with him.

"No," I said bluntly. "There better not be onions on that," I added, nodding at the pizza.

He grunted as we slipped through the hidden door that led to the ancient servants' quarters, and I followed him upstairs to Emma's old attic.

"Whoa!" he said, when he reached the top.

His reaction startled me, and I prepared myself for the worst, like discovering a nest of wraiths living up here. I readied my powers and burst into the room behind him.

Instead of ghosts, I found him staring at the painting leaning against the far wall, with a white sheet pooled around its base. It was the portrait of the first Emma, who looked just like me. Or, I guess, I looked just like her. She wore a French blue dress with tiny buttons down the front and a corseted bodice, and she looked slightly older than me, her eyes both steely and amused.

"God, Max, it's only a painting. I thought you'd discovered something."

"Sorry," he said. "But you have to admit it's bizarre."

I shook off my powers and removed a slice of pizza from the box. "Okay, yeah. Totally spooked me when I first saw it. It's like all the genes skipped five generations."

"Not all of them. *She's* beautiful."

"Jerk." I took a bite of pizza.

Max smiled as he cracked the bottle of Coke and took a swig. Then his expression grew more thoughtful. "How did we get here, Em?"

"I don't know." I stared at the portrait of my ancestor, wondering the same thing. "Is it all just fate?" I shook my head. "It doesn't matter. All we can do is end it."

He nodded, and I began the task of searching the crates, while Max moved a ladder around the room, inspecting the rafters for hidden holes. After a moment, I said, "Thanks, Max."

"It's only pizza."

"You know what I mean." I was thanking him for being here. For showing up when I needed him.

"Yeah, well, Mom and Dad would've killed me if I hadn't helped." Which is about as close as Max could get to saying, "you're welcome."

When I walked home that afternoon in the biting wind, I was dusty and exhausted, and wanted nothing more than a couple of Anatole's cookies and a hot shower. I had no idea where Natalie and Lukas were. I tried not to let it bother me, but it did. Last semester, the three of us were inseparable. Classes together, lunch, walking home after school, not to mention all the training and ghostkeeping. I missed Simon, too. Had he been the glue that held us together? Seemed unlikely that a twenty-eight-year-old Englishman who hated teenagers was our one common denominator, but I supposed there were stranger things.

Like seeing Bennett's Land Rover parked outside the museum. I stopped short, a sick feeling in the pit of my stomach. Was I excited at the prospect of seeing him, or worried that he'd look even worse and hate me for breaking up with him?

Probably a little of both.

I wavered at the gates, one foot on the sidewalk, the other in the gravel drive, debating my choices. My excitement at the thought of seeing him finally won out, and I practically ran the rest of the way home.

Bennett was waiting for me in the front hall, sitting on the bottom step of the grand staircase, playing with his phone. His buds were plugged into his ears and his head bounced to an inaudible rhythm.

He looked up when he heard me and my breath caught. He was skinny and ragged, his gray button-down shirt and tattered, faded jeans hanging off his frame, but I didn't care. I was so happy to see him, to fall into those blue eyes, even if they were ringed in red.

I smiled, tentatively at first, unsure how I'd be received. But he smiled, too. And slowly the smiles spread across our faces until we stood there, grinning like idiots, just so happy to see each other. I don't know who moved first, but we closed the distance, and then we were kissing. Until we heard a noise from another room. I stopped, staring wide-eyed at him. Were his parents going to interrupt us *again*?

But instead of pulling away from me, Bennett dragged me into the coat closet under the stairs, pressing me into the little space behind all the boots and jackets and hats. There was just enough room to stand, and we continued kissing, running our hands over each other's bodies, shutting out the world, only feeling, not seeing, until we finally felt reconnected and sure of each other.

"You don't hate me," he said, pleasure in his voice. I leaned against him, his hand resting in the small of my back.

I kissed him some more as I smiled. "Never."

He sighed contentedly, and held me tight a moment longer. Then he said, "I suppose we should get out of the closet."

"We can't just live here?" I cuddled into him. "It's all safe and warm. Everything's okay in here."

"How would we get food?"

"You don't eat," I said, reality already beginning to intrude.

"But you do," he said. "I suppose you could compel Anatole to cook and Celeste to bring you meals."

"Mmm, I'm hungry just thinking about it." I thought about the tea and cookies I'd planned on. "Come with me. I'll make you my special chai." I grabbed him by the hand and opened the door of the closet.

"Good," he said seriously. "I need to talk to you."

He scooped up his pack, followed me into the kitchen, and sat in the breakfast nook, watching me make us chai.

Anatole and Celeste were conspicuously absent, and I wasn't sure if I'd subconsciously compelled them to disappear, wanting the time alone with Bennett, or if they'd just recoiled from his Asarum-tinged power.

I remembered the first time we'd been in the kitchen together, after Bennett had dumped me alone in the museum with only the ghosts for company. Which in his mind was fine, because he thought I knew I was a ghostkeeper. I remembered how relieved I'd been when he'd reappeared a few mornings later, scowling at my minuscule, slutty uniform. And how pleased I'd been to know that he was secretly attracted.

What I didn't know was that it would all turn into *this*, this driving need to love him. Was it destiny? Or just that I only made sense in his arms, and he only made sense in mine? I loved my other guy friends—Coby and Harry and Lukas—but only Bennett made me feel like *this*.

I boiled the loose tea in a pan on the stove, and the smell of ginger and cinnamon permeated the room. I poured milk into two cups and used the steamer on the espresso machine to froth it. He smiled at me, and his smile made me a little dizzy—and I burned my finger on the steamer.

"Ow!"

Bennett jumped up from the nook and kissed my finger, then led me to the sink. I leaned against him, my back to his front, as he ran my hand under cold water. I could smell the chai, both familiar and foreign, and felt the heat of his body behind mine, the chill of the water on my fingers, as I melted into him.

I lifted my lips to his and we kissed like that until the tea almost boiled over on the stove and my fingers turned to ice. I poured the steeped tea into the frothy milk and added huge dollops of honey. I handed Bennett one of the mugs, and we sat together at the table, stirring our chais. We sat there for an hour, and he drank the whole cup of tea, which made me infinitely happy. But eventually I took his stained hand and asked, "Are you strong enough yet?"

He didn't answer for a moment, mourning the return to reality, I thought. Then he said, "To kill Neos? I'll never be strong enough to kill Neos, no matter how much Asarum I take."

"Then stop!"

He tucked my hair behind my ear. "Are *you* strong enough to dispel him?"

"I don't know, I—yes? No." I shook my head. "I've never really beat him, you know. I've never dispelled him, and this time—"

"Yes?"

"This time is the last." And I blurted the thing I'd been scared of, and had shared with nobody else. "What if he possesses me? What if I'm not strong enough to stop him? I don't even have my dagger."

To my surprise, he hardly reacted. "Emma, why can't you understand? I'm doing this because I won't let that happen."

It helped, having him say that. Helped me feel less scared. But it also made me wonder. I leaned against him as I asked, "Bennett, has it occurred to you that I'm not worth it? You're only twenty. There's got to be another girl out there who'd make you happy. And you wouldn't have to do this to yourself."

"There are only two things in my life that I'm sure of," he said. "One of them is you."

I was almost too afraid to ask. "What's the other?"

He gave me a look I couldn't decipher. "That what I'm doing is necessary."

"What? What's necessary? Is this—is this the secret Simon thinks you have? Tell me what you're planning."

He kissed me lightly. "I'm going back to the Knell. But when the time comes, I'll be here with you. It's going to be okay, Emma."

After he left, I thought about that final kiss. It didn't feel like he had a secret. It felt like he'd been saying good-bye.

14

I can't decide, Coby said. *Did he leave you happy or sad?* He was staring out my bedroom window at the front drive, and must have seen Bennett drive away.

A little of both, I admitted. Not wanting to discuss it, I said, *Did you manage to get closer to Neos? Learn anything new?*

The Beyond is weird. I can't get used to it. He gave me a look. *I'm glad I don't have to.*

Reminding me that he expected me to dispel him when this was all over. *Well, did you learn anything about his ashes? Or about Rachel? Did you see her?*

No, but they're together. At least, there are whispers of her—I can't tell if she's really with *him, or just along for the ride. You know how ghostkeepers get when they linger.*

Not really.

Crazy. Jumbled and confused, like a tangle of wires. But she wasn't lying, his ashes are definitely at Thatcher.

I sighed. This wasn't helping. *You don't know where?*

No, he admitted. *He wants to possess you, but he's afraid to attack you openly. He's got some plan with your ring and his ashes; they're like . . . symbols.*

Talismans, I said. *That's what they called my mother's amulet.*

Yeah. The ring will give him power, and I'm not sure, but I think he needs his ashes to possess you. You're Emma Vaile, he can't take you the normal way.

Ashes . . ., I said, lost in thought.

What? Coby drifted closer.

I almost told him about the vision with Neos and Bennett, but instead said, *It just reminds me of this dream I had in San Francisco before I had any idea I was a ghostkeeper. Of a smoky man made of snakes, inside my house; he was . . . The snakes were rising from my dad's collection of funeral urns.*

Your dad collects funeral urns?

I almost laughed at his expression. *He's an antiquities-dealing ghostkeeper. But that's not the worst part. When I brushed my teeth the next morning, there were ashes in my mouth.*

Like dead people's ashes? he asked. *That's just gross.*

No kidding. I still don't understand how they got there. I just hope the dream wasn't prophetic.

Do you get those? Coby asked. *Prophetic dreams?*

I thought about my vision in the Thatcher playing field, of Neos standing triumphant while Bennett drained my power. What was Bennett planning? *I hope not.*

I woke early, feeling antsy, and tossed and turned for a while. As I lay there thinking about ashes and dreams and

Bennett, I heard the faint hint of music. Sounded like a Bach cello piece, one of my dad's favorites. I got out of bed and followed the music down the hall, half hoping that my dad was surprising me with a visit.

The sound came from the open door of Mrs. Stern's office, and I stepped in, still wearing my flannel pj's. Mrs. Stern sat behind her desk, typing on her laptop. She was beautiful and imperious, wearing all black, her dark hair slicked back into its sleek ponytail. The thought of her checking her Facebook feed almost made me smile.

"Are you all right, Emma?"

"I heard the music and thought it was maybe my dad." I tried to give her a reassuring smile. "I'm fine."

She looked at me more closely. "Are you sure?"

"I—I don't know what to do, I—" Then I was crying, ugly gulping sobs that I expected would make her regret she'd ever asked the question.

Except she just said, "Oh, dear. Come here."

I went to her and she enveloped me in a hug. She led me to the yellow couch under the window and cradled me until I finally got the tears under control and settled into that weird hiccupping breathy noise you make when you're a little kid.

She handed me a tissue. "Do you want to tell me what's happened?"

I shook my head, then told her anyway. It helped to unload about my feelings for Bennett—even if it was a little weird telling his mother. And I explained I would never get over my guilt in Coby's death and that he wanted me to dispel him, and about being haunted—literally—by my dead aunt and the man who tried to kill me. "And all the kids at school. How am I supposed to keep them safe?"

"I don't know," she said, after a moment. "That all . . . sucks."

Enough that I wanted to stuff my face with comfort food. She caught me eyeing the breakfast tray on the coffee table. A white coffee cup held the remains of frothy milk and espresso, and there was one half-eaten croissant and another whole one.

"Are you hungry?" Mrs. Stern asked, offering me the plate.

"A little." I grabbed the croissant and took a perfect, flaky-buttery bite. "Oh, my God."

She smiled. "I know. Anatole gives me two, because he knows I love them."

"I'm sorry," I said around a mouthful. "I stole your second one."

"It's better this way." She ran a hand over her flat stomach.

Raised voices sounded in the hall; Natalie and Lukas were arguing over the bathroom. "It takes me five minutes to shower," Lukas grumbled. "You can't let me go in first?"

"Why should I?" Natalie said. "I was here first."

"Because you take forty minutes to get each strand of hair perfect, then you stare at yourself in the mirror for an hour."

"At least I don't spend that long over the three-course breakfast Anatole makes me special every morning."

"Why don't we just shower together?" Lukas snapped. "That's what you *used* to like."

"Shut! Up!" Natalie said, venomously.

I looked at Mrs. Stern. "And I thought all the fake politeness was bad. Should I go talk to them?"

"No," she said, standing. "I think that's my job."

She crossed to the door and leaned her head out. "Natalie, I just bought a shampoo that I'm not sure about. I'd love your opinion. Would you mind showering in our bathroom?"

Silence from the hallway.

"It's Aveda," Mrs. Stern tempted her.

"That would be wonderful," Natalie said politely, and I watched her sashay past the office door on her way to their bathroom.

"Thanks, Mrs. S," Lukas called out before slamming the bathroom door.

I stood, shoving another bite of croissant in my mouth. "I should get ready for school."

"Wait," Mrs. Stern said. "Sit down." She sat next to me and twisted her wedding ring in a circle around her finger. "I haven't been fair to you, Emma. It took me a long time to admit you weren't responsible for Olivia's death. And Bennett . . . well, I'd hoped your feelings for each other would fade, but they haven't, and I see now that they won't. His father and I made some unpopular choices ourselves."

"Mr. Stern's parents didn't want him losing his ghost-keeping powers?"

"Nobody wanted him to lose his powers," she said.

"Do you ever think you chose wrong?" I swallowed. "Does he?"

"I . . ." She glanced away, then turned back and clasped my hands. "You'll never get over the guilt. But you'll never get over the love, either."

I walked to school with Natalie. She didn't want to wait for Lukas to finish breakfast, so we'd started off together. It was snowing again, a light flurry that wasn't supposed to amount to much. I buttoned my coat and draped myself in the faux-fur hood. I liked how peaceful it felt. The snow seemed to muffle the ambient noise of the world, though not the crunching of the peanut-butter toast Celeste had handed Natalie at the door.

"It's good," she said around a mouthful. "Want a bite?"

"No, thanks. I already had one of Mrs. Stern's croissants."

She raised an eyebrow, and I told her about our conversation. "What did she mean, 'You'll never get over the love'? Why couldn't she just have said, 'Yeah, it's worth it'? Instead she leaves me totally confused about whether I want to feel guilty my whole life for stealing his powers or be miserable if I leave him, because I'll never stop loving him."

She crunched again. "Are you sure it's *his* powers that are going to get stolen?"

"What do you mean?"

"He's super-good at taking powers now, Em. That's part of what the Asarum does. What if he wants to take yours?" When I didn't answer, she said, "Don't pretend it never occurred to you."

I shrugged. "He wouldn't do that, not without asking me. He just wouldn't." I didn't mention my vision on the football field.

"Not before he started taking the herb. He's changed, Emma. Maybe he doesn't feel the same anymore."

"I don't know what he's planning, he won't tell me. But I do know he loves me, and I'll never stop loving him."

"How do you know that?" Natalie asked. "How can you be so sure? You're seventeen, Emma; you've only been together for a few months. What if he isn't *the one*?"

I grew silent as we crossed the street toward school, the soft snow falling all around us.

Natalie stopped and looked at the sky, the snowflakes dotting her face. "I'm asking because . . . I think I'm really in love with Lukas."

"Oh, Natalie." I hugged her. "I'm sorry."

"No," she said, pulling back from me. "That's just it. I do love him, but I don't think it's forever. Love's weird that way, you know?"

"Yeah," I agreed, but for different reasons. "Love's weird."

What I didn't say was that I didn't know why—maybe it was "destiny," or maybe it was something stronger and more ordinary—but I knew Bennett and I were *forever*.

Now I just had to figure out if I could live with taking all his powers. Or, if Natalie was right, with him taking mine.

We found Harry at the gates, buttoned up in his long black wool coat, brooding at his Droid. He looked up as we approached. "Natalie, *vos es decorus*.* Emma, you look like your dog died." He frowned. "Would it come back as a ghost?"

"I don't have a dog," I said repressively.

"In theory?" he asked.

"In theory," I answered, "this conversation sucks."

"Ignore her," Natalie told him. "She's grumpy about the never-ending saga of her and Bennett."

"*Natalie!*" I said. Did she have to share everything?

"What?" she asked. "Is that a secret?"

"No." I sighed. "I just want this to be over."

"You mean the thing with Bennett," Harry said slyly, no doubt trying to get a rise out of me.

"No. I mean Neos." It was true—it was time for me to end it, whatever it meant for me and Bennett. I'd allowed it to go on far too long.

In Latin class, I made a list of all the places we hadn't searched yet—or hadn't searched well enough. I actually wrote it in Latin, so if questioned by Mr. Z, I could say I was running vocab. Except in the end, the list looked more or less like: everywhere.

---

* You look beautiful.

I planned to do a little brainstorming during Advanced Bio, trying to narrow down the location from the other direction—who'd brought the ashes to Thatcher, and where would they have put them? But thoughts about what I was going to do to Neos when I did find him kept creeping in. Yeah, I wanted this to be over, but the final confrontation was bound to be ugly and bloody—I wasn't sure I was ready for that.

And today's assignment didn't help: dissecting a sheep's heart.

Really? I said to the universe. *I'm trying to track down a ghostly killer and you're tossing me a sheep's heart?*

In typical Thatcher fashion, the bio lab looked more like a high-tech kitchen than a high school science classroom. There were four counters made of stainless steel with square sinks cut into them, and I stood at one with my three lab partners, waiting for one of the guys to start cutting.

Instead, they both stood there making dumb jokes while the other girl nibbled her lower lip.

"Oh, give me the knife," I said.

I took the scalpel, eyed the worksheet, and made the incision. Not nearly as bad as a wraith—the sheep's heart didn't ooze black oil or leap up from the table to attack me. My partners took notes as I made the cuts and peeled back the flaps of flesh. When we got to the center, even the other girl was totally hooked.

"Wow," she said. "It's almost beautiful."

But I stepped back, dropping the scalpel in the sink.

Because the cold, dead flesh suddenly reminded me of Neos, of tearing his tongue from his mouth to get the jade amulet. What kind of person does that? The same kind of person who coldly cuts into a sheep's heart? I used to care. I used to worry about killing ghosts. Now I hardly even noticed, and I sliced into a sheep's heart like slicing a loaf of bread.

"I'm done," I said, and scrubbed my hands in the sink. Then I kept scrubbing, trying to wash away something deeper than the traces of sheep's heart.

One of the guys watching me said, "Who would've thought the old man had so much blood in him?"

My heartbeat spiked. This kid knew about Neos? Was he possessed? I spun on him and hissed, "*What* did you say?"

He stepped back in alarm. "Nothing! Nothing, it's a quote from *Macbeth*."

I exhaled. "Shakespeare?"

"Yeah, you were scrubbing your hands like Lady Macbeth after she forces her husband to kill the king. Chill out. It was only a joke."

I ignored him and wrote down my observations, but he was right. I was on edge. Even more than usual. I felt something coming, something cold and hard and big as a freight train, hurtling toward us from the darkness.

I stared at the scalpel in the bottom of the sink. Was I going to have to cut into Neos's heart before this all ended? How much blood would there be then?

15

There is a moment before a major storm when the world grows eerily quiet. Birds stop chirping, dogs quit barking, and families huddle in their houses. Conversations are hushed, and even the wind seems to slacken and wait.

There'd been no more possessions at school, no more outbursts at home. Natalie and Lukas were rebuilding a friendship. The Sterns were distant but kind. Bennett was nowhere, and even Harry and Sara were uncharacteristically quiet.

But with a storm, you know exactly where it's coming from. Clouds form, the wind lashes, and the sky goes gray—but no matter how hard I looked, I couldn't see Neos's attack coming.

So I lived my life. Went to class, searched the school grounds, and one night, alone in my room, called my mom again to ask her to come for Parents' Night.

"How's it going with the ashes?" was the first thing she asked.

"It's not," I said, hopping onto my bed. "The school's so old, there are too many hiding spots. For all we know, they're in a locker. Harry and Sara have been going to all the lounges, flirting and browbeating kids into letting them poke around, but there's still like three hundred to go—and that's just lockers."

"You don't sound hopeful," she said.

"We're not going to find the ashes," I told her. "Not before Neos comes."

"You feel it, too? The Knell is on high alert. Things are crazy here. Dad's going through Rachel's things, and he's not having a great time."

"What's wrong?"

"Nothing serious. Just reading things he'd rather not, and feeling guilty he wasn't there for her. He's hoping to find out why she's helping Neos. She helped him even before that wraith possessed her, you know. But why?"

"She loved him, isn't that enough?" I asked.

"No, Emma," Mom said. "It's not."

I sensed a lesson coming on, probably about Bennett, so I said, "I'm doing a presentation in Trig. For Parents' Night on Friday."

"Good. We'll be there."

"You will?" I couldn't keep the surprise out of my voice.

"Simon thinks whatever Neos is planning is going to happen in Echo Point. We're all coming up. We'll get there as soon as we can on Friday."

I was silent, trying not to let it bug me that they were

really coming because of Neos. Was it too much to ask that they act like normal parents for once? Although, I supposed they were trying to protect me, which *was* more important than solving a math problem in front of an audience.

My father muttered in the background and the phone thumped as my mother put her hand over it. But I still heard her muffled voice say, "No, I didn't forget . . . I know it's important . . . Fine. Then *you* tell her."

The phone clattered, and my dad came on the line. "Your mother has something to tell you," he said, and handed the phone back, with three random beeps, accidentally pressing buttons.

God. How hard was it to use a telephone? They were like cavemen at an ATM.

More scrambling, and my mother was back. "You know Simon's been researching the ashes? He's developed a theory. The ashes will increase Neos's strength and help him possess you."

"So, he'll be even stronger. Well, that's good news." I was terrified at the idea of Neos having more power.

"The good part is that Simon thinks the ashes will become noticeable to you a few minutes before Neos uses them. He can't hide them while he's preparing to use them. So once you feel the ashes, get them immediately."

"But no pressure, right?"

"Let's just hope it doesn't happen before we get there."

. . .

After hanging up with my mom, I crawled back to bed and stared at my homework for a while, but the words just swum around on the page. I thought about talking to Natalie or even Mrs. Stern, but what I really wanted was to break things. I went downstairs to spar with the Rake, but he didn't show, even though I waved my sword back and forth in the ballroom.

Instead, I replaced the sword and stomped into the billiard room and started whizzing balls around the pool table, making them smack into each other.

After a while, Natalie came and stood in the doorway. "You look like you've got a personal grudge against the fourteen ball."

"What's the fourteen ball ever done for me?" I smashed the three into it.

She stopped one of the balls from bouncing off the table. "Is this about Bennett?"

"No, it's about Neos. I just want this to be over."

She nodded. "Did Lukas tell you Simon called yesterday?"

"No. What'd he want?" To tell me I couldn't help Bennett? I creamed the fourteen with the yellow ball.

"To know if you've been feeling . . . what's the word he used?"

"Scared? Anxious? Panicked? Tense? *Emo*?"

"Foreboding!" she said, spinning the one ball across the table. "A sense of foreboding. Who talks like that?"

"Only Simon."

"Well . . . have you?"

"Yeah," I told her. "Whatever's coming, it's coming soon—and it's big."

The next two days crept past. Lukas never told me about Simon's call, I think because he didn't want to add to the feeling of growing dread. He and Natalie weren't polite or bickering anymore, both distracted by the gathering storm. Celeste was more formal and subdued than usual, Anatole bristled at everyone who stepped into his kitchen, and Mrs. Stern came across even more remote and chilly.

At school, Max searched the archives alone—Edmund had stopped appearing, and I didn't have the heart to summon him. Kylee was still acting timid and injured, and the ghost jocks were even more outrageously annoying—trying to cover their underlying nervousness, I thought.

Harry and Sara couldn't *feel* anything wrong, but they took their cues from us, and searched the student lounges with a wariness that I'd never seen from either of them. Britta was as sneering and mean as ever, completely unchanged, and I wanted to kiss her.

I managed to restrain myself.

After dinner on Friday, I changed into my gray boatneck sweater, red pashmina, black miniskirt, thick tights, and my favorite boots, and stepped into the hall.

"Well," Lukas said. "If it isn't the Great Unparented."

He and Natalie met me at the top of the stairs, ready to face Parents' Night without parents. It was freezing outside, so even Lukas had resorted to a long-sleeve brown polo over jeans, while Natalie wore her leopard-print sweater, because she liked wearing it into battle, and that's how she viewed tonight.

"I thought your parents were coming," Natalie said.

I shrugged. "I thought so, too. Just once, it would be nice to be able to rely on them showing up."

We stood there for a moment, looking at each other with recognition. We weren't the center of our parents' lives. And maybe that was okay.

"Don't laugh," I said, "but I love you guys."

So, of course, they both started cracking up.

"I said *don't* laugh." I giggled along with them, partly from the break in the tension. "I'm serious. You're the best friends I've ever had, and . . . and screw them. Our parents. Screw them for being screwed up."

"Yeah," Natalie said. "*They're* messed up. We rock!"

"I feel like I'm at a pep rally," Lukas said, shaking his head, but I could tell he was pleased. "Let's go meet the snobs."

"You think their parents are going to be snobs?" I asked.

"He meant the kids," Natalie said.

"Oh, right." The three of us would always be something a little different, never quite fitting in. "At least there's Harry and Sara."

"Yeah," she said. "They're too rich to be snobs."

I felt a little guilty for laughing, but it was kind of true. Too rich to bother snubbing anyone.

Downstairs in the foyer, we discovered Mr. and Mrs.

Stern putting on their coats. Mrs. Stern was dressed in a charcoal gray satin blouse and black pants, and Mr. Stern in a navy suit.

"You're going out?" I asked.

"It's Parents' Night, isn't it?" Mr. Stern grumbled. "Hate these things."

"John," Mrs. Stern said warningly.

He glanced at us apologetically. "Oh, right. Should be fun."

"What—because you're on the board?" Natalie asked. "You don't have kids there anymore."

Mrs. Stern wrapped a black cashmere scarf around her neck. "We have you, don't we?"

Natalie and Lukas and I all looked at each other. We had one of those mind-meld moments, when you know what your friends are thinking—because you're thinking the same thing. Maybe our parents had failed, but we had the Sterns, and that wasn't nothing.

"I hope one of you is presenting," Mr. Stern said, breaking the short silence. "At least that breaks the tedium."

"Trig," I answered.

"Fencing," Natalie murmured.

"I got stuck with Latin," Lukas said morosely.

"Emma, you didn't get fencing?" Mr. Stern grinned. "Color me surprised."

I smiled back, and we shuffled to the freezing garage and into their Porsche Cayenne. I sat in back between Natalie and Lukas, like a buffer zone. They were learning how to be "just friends" again, but I got the impression sometimes they were one smoldering look away from falling off the wagon.

At least it was a short drive and I was toasty.

Then Mrs. Stern cleared her throat. "Natalie, I . . . I should've said something earlier, but I didn't know how to tell you."

"Uh-oh," Natalie said.

"You are so busted," Lukas told her.

"I didn't *do* anything!" she said. Then, a little quieter, "I don't think."

Mrs. Stern turned around in the front passenger seat. "I knew your mother. Before she left the Knell. We were friends."

Natalie frowned, like she couldn't imagine her mother knowing the sleek, wealthy Mrs. Stern. "You and my mom?"

"It's a small community," Mrs. Stern explained. "For a few years, we were very close."

"What happened?"

Mrs. Stern put her hand on Mr. Stern's arm. "Boys."

"You mean because my dad wouldn't let her hang with you anymore?" Natalie asked. "How could she abandon a friend for a *guy*?"

"Yeah," Lukas said sarcastically. "What was she thinking?"

I jabbed him with my elbow and whispered, "Not about you, Lukas."

"It's never about me," he grumbled, but he shut up.

"We're in the parking lot, Alex," Mr. Stern said. "If you're going to tell her, tell her now."

Mrs. Stern bit her lip. “I haven’t seen her for a long time, but . . . your mother may be here tonight. I called her.”

I waited for Natalie to explode, but instead she looked like a frightened deer. I couldn’t remember her ever being at a loss for words. I grabbed her hand and squeezed tight.

“How could you do that?” Lukas snapped at Mrs. Stern, then turned to Natalie. “You don’t have to see her. I’ll walk you home.”

“Me, too,” I said. “Whatever you want.”

“I called to tell her you were with me,” Mrs. Stern told Natalie. “And how wonderful you’d turned out—how proud she should be of you. We don’t know what’s going to happen with Neos. I didn’t want her to lose you before she saw you again. I know what that feels like.” She tried to shake away the loss of Olivia, and Mr. Stern laid a comforting hand on her thigh. “Anyway, I told her it was Parents’ Night. I’m sorry if I did the wrong thing.”

“You think?” Lukas said. “After the way she treated Natalie—”

“It wasn’t her,” Natalie said in a small voice. “She called the Knell to help me. Do I have to go back with her?”

“Of course not,” Mr. Stern said reassuringly. “You’ll stay with us as long as you like.”

“She only wants to see you, Natalie,” Mrs. Stern said. “If you’d rather not, we’ll all go home.”

“You don’t have to,” I told Natalie.

She took a deep breath and told me, “You’re not the only one who’s tough around here.”

“You’re right.” I grinned at her. “Let’s go get her.”

"Emma," Mrs. Stern cautioned.

"I mean *meet* her," I said innocently, as Lukas fist-bumped me in the dark.

Inside Thatcher's front hall, a group of sophomore girls stood at the door, answering questions and handing out programs. The immense room was pretty at night, with the chandelier glowing, the marble floors polished, and a fire roaring in the hearth, illuminating the stairway and hanging tapestries. Gorgeous bouquets dotted the room, overshadowing the huge silk flower centerpiece, and the faint strains of classical music played, barely audible above the chatter of conversation.

Lukas made straight for the banquet table, while the Sterns mingled among the other parents. Natalie and I found a relatively quiet corner to check our names in the programs and search for her mother.

"Do you see her?" I asked, folding my program closed.

"We're scheduled at the same time," Natalie said, ignoring my question. "We can't go to each other's presentations."

"It's not too late to leave before she gets here."

"I'll be nervous without you."

"Natalie, stop avoiding the subject."

"Maybe she won't come," she finally said, but I couldn't tell if that would be a good thing or bad.

She scanned the crowd for her mother, and I did the same, struck again by how *eastern* everyone looked. A bunch of rich parents in California would've looked completely different: skinnier, more casual and athletic. Instead of fake-tanning and visiting personal trainers, Thatcher parents tended more toward fine dining and art openings.

Then a woman came through the front doors, looking a little jet-lagged and a lot out of place. Her steel gray hair was fixed in a long braid down her back, and she removed a full-length brown parka, revealing a long brown skirt and boxy pink sweater. But as she spoke to the sophomore girls, the light caught her profile, and there was something familiar there.

"Is that her?" I asked, pointing.

Natalie caught her breath. "Yeah."

"She looks . . . sort of sweet."

Natalie shot me a look.

"Sorry, I didn't mean that."

She gave me another look.

"Unless, you want me to mean it?"

Natalie let out a noise of frustration. "Let's just go talk to her."

She grabbed my hand and dragged me through the crowd. She stopped in front of her mother, who had moved toward the fireplace, and said, "You came."

Her mother's face seemed to crumble. "Should I not have?"

Up close, I saw she'd once been beautiful, like Natalie, but at the moment she just looked exhausted and unsure. And the usually self-confident Natalie was frowning silently at the floor.

"I don't want to embarrass you in front of your friends," her mother said.

"*Embarrass* me?" Natalie said. "Is that what you think?"

"I don't know what to think," her mother said in a small voice.

Natalie just shook her head, and the two of them stood there, miserable and silent.

I scanned the room, but couldn't find the Sterns or Lukas. And I shouldn't *have* to find them. This was Natalie's mother—she should be the person *helping* Natalie in an awkward situation like this, not the person who *caused* the awkwardness. And when I thought about that, I found it inexcusable. She'd sent her fantastic daughter to live with strangers, defenseless, traumatized, and alone.

Okay, maybe my feelings were partly meant for my own parents, but I was still really pissed off for Natalie. I clenched my fists, flushed and livid, and snapped at her mother. "What is *wrong* with you? How could you have sent Natalie away? Don't you know how special she is? How much she needed you? Then you show up at Parents' Night, like that's really who you are? You don't deserve to have people think you made this beautiful, strong, amazing girl."

A few heads turned at my raised voice, but before I could continue, Max appeared at my elbow. "You'll have to forgive my sister," he said to Natalie's mom. "She's a pit bull."

I glared at him. "What are you doing here?"

"See what I mean?" he asked Natalie's mom.

"Shut up," I told him.

"Mom told me to come," he explained. "Because they're late."

"Typical." Though I was glad they hadn't forgotten. "Anyway, you're not exactly parental. The Sterns came—at least they're good parents."

"Right," he said. "That's why Bennett gets along with them so well."

"Are you purposely goading me?"

"Yes." He pulled me away from Natalie and her mother. "Emma, let Natalie work this out for herself."

I glanced back at Natalie. "She needs me."

Then Mrs. Stern slipped through the crowd and took Natalie's mother in a hug and said, "The three of us should find someplace quieter."

I started to follow, but Max took my elbow. "Let them go."

"I have to go with them." Instead of subsiding, my anger had turned into agitation. I wanted to pace or scream—something just wasn't right.

"I'll handle this, Emma," Mrs. Stern said.

"But you're not pissed off enough," I protested.

"I am," Lukas said, stepping around Mrs. Stern. "I'll go."

16

Despite her dumping him, I knew Lukas still cared about Natalie and that he'd take care of her, so I let Max drag me to the other side of the great hall. But instead of calming down, my skin began to crawl. What I thought had been agitation over Natalie and her mother crystallized into something else.

Neos was here. Somewhere near this crowded room, amid the chatter and the clinking glasses, the cracking of the fire and the faint strains of violin, I sensed the scratchy, unearthly whisper of his wraiths.

I froze in place, drawing my power around myself like a cloak, my gaze flitting through the milling crowd, terrified I'd spot the inky tattered flesh of a wraith. I could almost taste Neos in the air, rancid and poisonous.

He felt close as the crowd surged around me, and I probed with my powers, searching for him. "Do you feel that?" I whispered to Max.

"I feel *you*," he said. "What're you doing?"

"Neos is here." The moment I said the words, I realized I was wrong. "No, he's not. His ashes. I'm feeling his ashes."

Power sparked inside Max, and he turned business-like. "Where?"

"I don't know, it's still muffled."

Then we both felt it. An eruption of spectral hunger and rot that sent malevolent echoes throughout the room. Max pointed toward one of the back hallways. "There?"

"Yeah. I thought it was closer, but . . ." I shook my head. "You get the others, I'll go ahead."

"By yourself?"

"Simon said we had to be fast. We've got maybe fifteen minutes," I said. "Go!"

Max said, "If you get hurt, I'll kill you," then started shouldering through the crowd toward the door through which the others had disappeared.

I weaved through a bunch of parents drinking wine. The sense of being surrounded by Neos's power stayed with me, but I kept my focus on the strongest eruption of nastiness and followed it into the hallway.

When the door closed behind me, the noise and heat of the main hall became muffled. My hand moved to my hip, but of course I had no dagger.

"Okay, Emma," I said in the deserted hallway. Not just to myself, but to the other Emma. This was *her* house; her power still resonated through these walls. And yeah, maybe Neos had staged every step of this fight, but that had to count for something.

My spine tingled so sharply that it felt like pinpricks.

I drew my power into my arms and my clenched fists. This wasn't just Emma's house—this was mine: my school, my friends. My life. And I wasn't going to let Neos take it from me.

The clattering of my heels sounded flat and lonely in the corridor as I crept toward the spectral stench. I passed the first two student lounges, the doors to the computer lab, and one of the classrooms, and came to the end of the hallway, where I found a dark stain on the floor. Except that was no stain, that was an inky-black shadow, a shadow with no source, cast by no light.

It was a rip in the veil between the worlds. My power swirled around me as wraiths poured out of the Beyond. Three of them, insectoid and famished, with tattered skin and insatiable hunger. Their whispers almost deafened me: *Neos, Neos, crack the skin and suck the flesh.* They rushed me, bony claws grasping, gaping mouths spitting acid.

I smiled as my power flowed around me until I was covered with a translucent layer of energy, compelling and dispelling magic swirling together. I backhanded the first wraith and it burst into shards.

The second wraith lunged for my throat and I sidestepped, spun, and elbowed it in the back of the neck. A spectral joint snapped and the second wraith dissolved. The third wraith hesitated, hissing and spitting.

A ray of power shot from my fingertips, melting it into a black tarry stain on the floor. But it wasn't dead. The tarry stain thickened and grew and took the form of a child—a little blond girl who stared at me with big, pleading eyes.

But I'd met this kind of wraith before, and I wasn't going to waste any tears this time. She crawled toward me, inky tendrils sprouting from her fingernails, and I blasted her into dust.

Her death seemed to trigger a reaction. More wraiths boiled from the Beyond, maybe a dozen of them—hard to tell where one ended and the next began. I kneed one wraith in the face and twisted another like a dishrag as I heard footsteps running toward me from behind. Max yelled, "The ashes, Em! Where are the ashes?"

Oh, God. I'd gotten so caught up in killing wraiths, I'd forgotten. "I don't know—not here."

"Find them," Lukas said. "We've got this."

Following him and Max were Natalie and the Sterns—and Natalie's mom, looking terrified but willing. As a group, they rushed toward me, bristling with ghostkeeping powers. Natalie and her mother held hands and Natalie used her reverse-summoning power to banish a wraith, which she'd never been strong enough to do before—she was directing her mother's power, too. When Natalie and I held hands, we always interfered with each other, but she and her mother seemed to work together on some instinctive level.

"This is why, Natalie," her mother cried. "This is why I didn't want this life for you."

"This *is* why," Natalie yelled back triumphantly, banishing another wraith. "Why I love it!"

Then Lukas plowed into a bunch of wraiths, parting them like Moses parted the Red Sea—slamming half against one wall and half against the other, while Max and Mrs. Stern started ripping into them. Mr. Stern hung back—unable to see the wraiths, but ready to rush in and drag anyone away if necessary, which struck me as the bravest thing of all.

They looked pretty good, but that was a lot of wraiths, and I wasn't sure they could win. Actually, I was pretty sure they couldn't.

"Neos sent these as a distraction," Mrs. Stern told me. "To keep you from finding the ashes."

I still hesitated. What if they lost because I left them?

"Don't let him win," Natalie told me. "Move your butt, Emma."

She was right. I had to trust them. I backpedaled, and while the wraiths howled and snapped and swarmed after me, the others held them back.

Fifty feet down the hallway, with the sound of the battle echoing behind me, I sensed another source of Neos's power. It came from the main hall, a dull throb of anger and hate. Crap. We'd left the students and their parents totally defenseless.

When would my parents get here? They could be helping. And where the hell was Bennett? He promised he'd be here.

I ran, bursting through the doors into the main hall, full of heat and noise. Then I stopped. Nothing looked different, but everything felt wrong.

The ashes were here. In the main hall. They'd *always* been here.

Except I still couldn't tell where, exactly. I side-stepped through the crowd, ignoring everyone, my powers stretched to the limit, as I closed in on the ashes. Then a hand grabbed my elbow from behind.

I stomped backward on the person's foot, then spun to elbow them in the throat, and Sara yelped. "*Ow*! Ow-ow-ow!"

"And *that*," Harry said, reaching to steady her as she hopped, "is why I never dance with Emma. Those monkey toes of hers are dangerous."

"The ashes are *here*," I whispered, as the spectral energy thickened in the air. "And . . ."

"And what?" Sara said, rubbing her foot.

I turned my back to the crowd. "Ghosts. Lots of ghosts."

"Good ghosts?" Harry asked hopefully. "Like Casper?"

"Don't make a face," I told them. "But they're possessed. I think, like, a quarter of the people in the room."

So, of course, Harry loudly said, "Seriously?" and scanned the crowd.

Sara slugged him in the stomach, and as he bent over in pain, I scream-whispered into his ear. "They'll come after us if they know we know, you idiot."

People eyed us suspiciously, and I felt a shiver of fear at the thought of Neos inside one of those bodies. What would I do if they all jumped us at once?

"There's no way you saw Matt Damon," Harry said, even louder than before, trying to cover his mistake. "His kids aren't old enough for high school."

"I said he *looked* like Matt Damon."

Harry shot me a superior look. "Remember that time you thought you saw Lady Gaga, but it was only a large poodle?"

I mumbled something in reply, trying to watch the crowd and summon my powers without attracting too much notice. The possessed people stopped paying attention to us, but how long could *that* last? They must know who I was. What were they waiting for?

It didn't matter. I needed to find the ashes. I felt them nearby, but the ghostly auras of the possessed people interfered with my ability to pinpoint them. Maybe that was why Neos wanted them possessed.

I looked at the tapestries, the furniture, the hearth—and saw Coby, solidifying in the air behind Harry and Sara. The other ghosts didn't seem to notice him—just one more ghost in the crowd—but he must've been worried that if he talked to me he'd attract attention, because he just hovered over them, his face grave and eyes urgent.

I got the message. I needed to get rid of Harry and Sara before they were possessed, too.

"It's almost time for my presentation," I said brightly. "Meet me in the classroom?"

"Math?" Harry asked, apparently still thinking I was trying to pretend everything was all right, instead of trying to get them out of there. "I want a cookie first."

"Harry," Sara said, through clenched teeth. "Let's go."

She'd always seemed sensitive to ghosts, especially

Coby, and she hooked her arm through Harry's and started dragging him through the crowd.

Which was growing quieter and quieter as more people were possessed. A moment ago, a quarter of them—now, half. The dean stood slouching and sneering near the fire, a wineglass forgotten in her hand. Mr. Jones swayed in place, his eyes blank, licking his lips as two junior girls nattered at him, totally clueless.

I circled through the quieting crowd, tracking the ashes like a bloodhound after a scent. I felt the murderous attention of the people in the room on the back of my neck, and prayed that as long as I pretended I didn't know they were possessed, they wouldn't attack.

But what if they did? How was I supposed to beat back a mob? I'd only be able to dispel a few before the rest of them swarmed me. Even if I had my dagger, I wouldn't have been willing to hurt any of these people. They weren't my enemies; they were Neos's victims.

I swallowed nervously, willing myself to continue. But as we passed the room's massive fireplace, a bed of ashes and burning embers began to stir in the grate. A spectral breeze swirled as a figure took shape.

Rachel materialized in the air and looked directly at me. *You're too late, Emma. He has your ring. He has the ashes.*

Where are they? I asked her. *Rachel, please help me! You're my only hope.*

The mad Ophelia expression on her face was even more pronounced than ever. Any sanity she'd shown when she'd appeared to me before was gone. *I'm sorry, Emma.*

He's the only one who can save me from eternal unrest. I know he's . . .

Evil, I said. *Is that the word you're looking for?*

I love him, she said fiercely. *No matter what he's become.*

He can't save you, he can't—

He already has. Love is my afterlife, Emma. She beamed madly at me.

You're losing your mind, Rachel. Listen to yourself. Look what you're doing—look what you've done. Neos isn't the only one who can save you. Tell me where the ashes are, and I'll help you. I'll end your suffering. I can do that, Rachel; I can put you to rest.

You mean kill me. Her eyes flashed with sudden menace. *He told me not to trust you. That you were just like your mother.*

I drew on my compelling powers—I'd *make* her tell me where the ashes were. *I'm sorry, Rachel, but—*

Hands grabbed me from behind. The dean and a visiting father grabbed my left hand and Mr. Z and some senior kid grabbed my right, while someone's mother held me tight around the neck.

Rachel drifted toward the table in front of the hearth. With a sweep of her arm, she sent three arrangements of cut flowers crashing to the floor, leaving only the silk flower centerpiece. *They're right here, Emma, hidden in plain sight.* She yanked the artificial flowers from the pot, and pulled a plain cardboard box from beneath.

She raised the box of ashes and opened her mouth as if to call for Neos—and then everything happened at once.

I released a blast of dispelling energy—not just from my hands but from my whole body—that coiled into the ghosts inside the people holding me and reduced them to dust. But before I had a chance to focus on Rachel, more hands grabbed me as the crowd of possessed people surged forward in waves.

At the same time, Harry hopped the couch, snatched the box from Rachel's hand, and shouted, "Dude, you *have* no ashes."

I had to admire Harry's bravery, thinking he was taunting Neos, given all he'd seen was a cardboard box hanging in midair. When he raced toward the door, the ghosts shrieked and surged, terrified of losing the ashes. They grabbed and tore at me; I summoned and dispelled them until one of my bio lab partners socked me in the face.

I went down hard, but still managed to summon the ghost from the kid's body. It was a leather-clad biker with a shaved head, who apparently hadn't worn his helmet, because his skull was cracked on one side. If I'd met him on a dark street after midnight, I might have been scared, but now I just zapped him with a bolt of dispelling energy and watched him crumble.

Harry sped for the exit, galloping like a gawky colt. He didn't get far before a ghost slammed into him. Not a possessed person, a disembodied ghost. The box of cardboard sailed through the air, and Harry stumbled, then stiffened. He turned toward me as the ghost filtered into his body, and an alien expression rose on his face.

Harry was possessed.

I cried out as my gaze followed the box through the air, and for a moment I felt a flash of hope. There! Sara was right in its path. But in the same moment that she caught the box, I realized she'd been possessed, too.

The ghosts recognized one of their own, and stopped worrying about the ashes. Instead, they just worried about me. As they marched toward me, I summoned a Depression-era-looking guy from Mr. Jones, a pilgrim woman from a freshman boy, and a hippie wearing serious bell-bottoms and an orange suede vest from someone's mom and melted them all into oily grease marks on the carpet. Thatcher's orientals would never be the same.

But they were about to overwhelm me.

As fast as I was, I couldn't dispel them all, not before they buried me beneath a mound of hitting, kicking, biting bodies.

Except they didn't. One of them punched my mouth and I stumbled backward, seeing stars—then the rest of them began screeching again and turned toward Sara.

She was cradling the box of ashes under one arm like a football and racing toward the side door. I couldn't understand—she was clearly possessed, but trying to get the ashes *away* from Rachel.

Three possessed students lunged at her, and despite her dress and heels, she did this fake-left-lunge-right thing that left them on the ground. One of the possessed janitors loomed in front of her, and she slammed into him with her shoulder, sending him sprawling, and kept running. She scrambled to the door and seemed to spin in place, then threw the box of ashes in a perfect spiral that ended, almost magically, in my arms.

That's when I realized—she was possessed by Coby!

I dodged the grasping hands, crawled under the buffet table, and stood up to break for the staircase when Harry loomed in front of me. I summoned a guy who looked like an extra on *Mad Men* from his body and dispelled him without a thought.

Harry swooned and almost fainted before draping one arm around me. "Wha—?" he said.

"We're running away," I told him, and dragged him toward the door.

I wouldn't have made it if Craven and Moorehead hadn't appeared from nowhere.

Barfight! Craven called.

Cowabunga! Moorehead said.

I could always count on them for team spirit as they leaped into the melee, hurling themselves at the pursuing ghosts. And so did—

Edmund? I gasped.

He'd wrapped his arms around Coach's muscular legs, catching the ghost inside her, his brown suit crazily disarranged. *Stop dilly-dallying!* he told me. *Get moving!*

Good advice. Except with Harry leaning on me and the ashes in one hand, I couldn't really fight—and there were just as many possessed people as ever. Every time I dispelled one ghost, another took its place. I summoned and blasted them, and a minute later, another slipped into the same body. I couldn't stop the ghosts without hurting the people they were inside—and that was one line Neos would never make me cross.

Still, I summoned and dispelled and sidled toward the staircase, with Moorehead, Craven, and a bedraggled Edmund—and now Sara—beside me. I kept thinking that maybe Natalie and Lukas and the others would appear, but they didn't. Either they were still fighting the wraiths . . . or they'd lost.

We started retreating upstairs, but the onslaught was too much. Craven was getting pummeled by a goth chick—which, if I survived this, I'd never let him forget—and Edmund was repeatedly hitting a banker-looking dad in the fist with his stomach.

Sara gasped, "Get those ashes away, Emma. We'll keep them here for as long as we can."

"Which of you is that?" I asked. "Is Coby still inside you?"

"It's both of us," she said, tossing the goth chick over the stair railing. "Now *go*!"

"No way. I'm not leaving without—"

"We're here!" Simon yelled, bursting through the front door. His long camel-hair coat swung with action and his glasses glinted in the light of the chandelier. For once he looked pretty powerful, as he dispelled three ghosts with rapid-fire blasts.

"Simon!" I cried out.

"What took you so long?" Harry grumbled, leaning against the banister and pulling himself upstairs.

"Traffic was a bitch," Simon quipped, then zapped another ghost.

For the first time all night, I smiled. Good to have him back—and to see my parents hustling in behind him. Simon hammered the ghosts from behind, and after I handed Sara/Coby the ashes, I helped from the base of the stairs.

My dad started pummeling a chubby, mutton-chopped ghost with his fists.

"What are those?" I asked, glancing at the thick, quilted gloves that were protecting his hands from ghostbite.

"A little idea I cooked up," he said. "Barbecue mitts. Nothing can eat through these babies." He looked like some weathered old cop as he punched another ghost in the mouth.

Now him, *I like*, I heard Moorehead say.

They don't make 'em like that anymore, Craven agreed.

"Mom!" I called. "Watch out!"

She couldn't even see the ghosts, but apparently she'd come prepared to deal with possessed people. She spun and squirted pepper spray in a student's eyes. Then, clearly impressed by the results, she squirted an arc in front of her, until she joined us on the stairs.

"Where's Bennett?" I asked.

"Who knows?" Simon told me. "I left him a dozen messages."

"Um, honey?" My father glanced at the possessed people massing below, then at me. "Is there a plan?"

I looked upstairs and saw Harry at the double doors leading into the hallway. "Yeah. *Run.*"

17

We got through the doors and my dad and mom slammed them shut while Simon and I kept the approaching mob at bay with bursts of dispelling power. Harry, still barely conscious, shoved the doorstop into place, but ghosts shot directly through the doors, from every era and in every costume.

Then the pounding began. The possessed people on the other side slammed into the doors, which creaked and groaned.

"I'm afraid that won't keep them back for long," Simon said.

And I'm not kidding, my mom said, "Ya *think*?"

Simon flushed, and my dad draped Harry's arm across his shoulder and we rushed down the hallway, away from the shuddering doors. We were a motley group of ghosts and the living. My dad supported Harry, and my mother stepped right through Edmund without noticing; Coby, now out of Sara, directed the ghost jocks, and Sara stuck close to Simon.

Neos is here, Edmund told me.

Obviously, I said, pausing to dispel two ghosts that were following us.

How are you going to stop him? he asked, his face concerned.

Edmund, I didn't know you cared.

It's not something to joke about, Emma.

I'm not sure, okay? I'm going to stop him, that's all. I don't know how.

We rounded the corner and stopped short when we saw them: a pack of seniors, all boys, all possessed, all dressed in pastel cashmere sweaters and skinny jeans. They looked like some preppy gang, as though we were in the ghost-world version of *West Side Story.*

They spread out, covering the width of the hallway as they stalked forward. I knew Simon and I could take them, but I wasn't so sure we could protect the non-ghostkeepers. Especially when I heard the sound of the locked doors splintering and crashing open behind us, then the footsteps of the possessed mob.

I needed a place to hide Harry and Sara and my parents until this was over. The auditorium or the teacher's lounge or—there! A custodian's closet across the hall.

I tried the knob. Locked.

I'm on it, Coby said, and put his hand into the door and fiddled around until I heard a *click.*

I smiled at him; he always knew what I was thinking.

But I'd lowered my guard for one moment too long, and as the possessed preppies approached from the front, the ghost of what looked like a wholesome farm boy—except for the vicious grin—rose from the floor and lunged at Harry.

My dad swung at him, but the ghost caught his arm and slammed him into the wall, then dove at Harry again. But Edmund jumped in front of Harry and took the full brunt of the farm boy's attack.

I left the pastel posse for Simon as I tried to help Edmund. He and the farm boy were rolling around, fists flying like a cartoon fight, and I couldn't get a lock on the farm boy.

"Emma!" Simon called. "A little help?"

I glanced over and found him almost lost in the pastel onslaught. I compelled the possessed boys away, to give Simon time to dispel them, and when I looked back, the farm boy was using Edmund as a shield against me.

Caught in the farm boy's grip, Edmund fixed me with his eyes. *It's time. Dispel us both. Do as you promised.*

He was right. It was time. *I'll miss you*, I told him, and fired a quick burst of dispelling energy.

As he and the farm boy faded into dust, Edmund's voice rang in my head. *I always thought you were rather marvelous, Emma Vaile. Live well.*

Simon finished off the other ghosts, leaving a bunch of semiconscious pastel seniors in a heap on the floor, and I stood staring at the empty hallway where Edmund should've been. The man in the brown suit was gone.

"Thank you, Edmund," I said to his dust. "For everything."

"What's going on?" Harry asked from where he lay in a heap on the floor.

"You're going in the closet." I turned to my parents. "You, too. Everyone who can't fight."

Sara gave Simon the ashes, then led Harry into the closet. My dad said, "I can fight," then staggered a step, still dizzy from the farm boy's attack. "Oh."

My mother took his hand. "Emma's right, Nathan. We'd just be in the way."

"Hey," I told them. "At least you got here."

As I closed the door, I said to Coby, *You and the boys stay here and watch over them. I can't keep going if I don't know they're safe.*

You stay. I'm going with her, Coby told Moorehead and Craven.

Oh no, Craven said, mock-regretfully. *We can't fight Neos and his wraiths? We were so looking forward to that.*

The door opened a crack, and a groggy Harry peered into the hallway. "We should come with you, we can—"

"Namaste, Harry," I said, slamming and locking the door. "Nama-*stay*!"

The pounding footsteps of the mob sounded closer, and then the first of them skidded around the corner.

Simon peppered them with dispelling energy, and I loosed a blast, but they didn't slow. Three people just collapsed, and the rest of the mob stampeded over them.

"That's bad," Simon said. "They could kill them."

I nodded. "Yeah, I don't know—"

We need to lead them away from the closet, Coby interrupted. *Time to run.*

I tried compelling the mob, sending power over my shoulder, as I led Coby and Simon in a mad dash back toward the main hall.

Along the way, we battled ghosts, possessed people, and wraiths, but we got there. And then we saw them. Max, Mrs. and Mr. Stern, Lukas, Natalie, and her mom.

A wave of relief washed over me, and I ran toward them. "Hey!"

But when we got close, they turned, and I saw they were bruised and bleeding, their hair crazy and their clothes ripped. And their eyes were wrong.

Possessed. All of them.

Before I could react, Mrs. Stern slugged me in the stomach, and I gasped and folded as Lukas kicked my legs out from under me and Natalie punched me in the ear. I hit the ground hard, and barely saw Natalie's mom knee Simon before Max took him in a headlock and punched him in the face.

These were my best friends. The people I trusted most. The people who knew me best, and who loved me anyway. And they'd been turned into Neos's puppets. He could do nothing to hurt me more.

Coby dove to rescue me, but a dozen ghostly hands reached from under the floor and grabbed him, trapping and pummeling him.

I lay on the floor, trying to figure out what to do. I felt abandoned and alone and weak, like we'd already failed.

Then Rachel appeared at the top of the stairs. *The ashes! Get the ashes and bring them to Neos.*

Simon fought hard, but he couldn't summon his dispelling power through the shock and pain. I knew, because I was the same. Natalie's mom plucked the ashes from his coat pocket and rushed the box to Rachel. I started to compel her to stop, but Lukas moved to kick me, his face a sneering stranger's.

That's when my anger caught fire. It burned brighter and brighter and finally snapped, going from red-hot to ice-cold.

I compelled with one word: *Go.*

The explosion of power burst from me with the force of a grenade. As the ghosts ripped from their bodies, Lukas, Natalie, her mother, Max, and the Sterns collapsed—leaving me and Simon in the center of a circle of unconscious bodies. Even Coby had disappeared.

But I couldn't worry about him, because Rachel still had the ashes. And before I could stop her, she fled down the hall.

I helped Simon to his feet and looked at the limp bodies. "Are they going to be all right?"

"I don't know," was his not-very-reassuring response. "Each possession is different. We've got to stop Rachel before she brings those ashes to Neos."

We climbed the stairs, fending off new ghosts and possessed students and parents.

"He's trying to make you angry," Simon said.

"It's working."

18

"He's inside," I told Simon. I could feel Neos's sick energy throbbing behind the closed doors of the research library that we'd tracked Rachel to.

"You know it's a trap," he replied. "He planned this whole thing."

"Yeah." I pushed through the doors, wishing I had someone with me other than Simon. He was a smart and fearless leader, but he wasn't that strong, and right now I needed someone with some kick-butt abilities. And, well, I'll admit it: part of me expected Bennett to arrive in the nick of time to help me save the day.

What I didn't expect was to open those doors and find him already locked in deadly combat. He stood on the long mahogany table in the center of the room, a spear of brilliant white light in each hand, power rippling from him in pounding waves. He looked gorgeous and heroic as a sea of wraiths boiled around him, a mass of ripping claws, gaping mouths, and tattered skin.

Bennett seemed to know where they were without looking, one spear slicing through a wraith behind him, then two in front, another spear flashing as he spun and kicked. He fought in silence, without mercy or hesitation, until he saw his chance—he leaped from the table and raced up a spiral staircase that led to a gallery around the room.

I think I shouted Bennett's name, but I'm not sure. Ghosts came from behind us and surged forward. I dispelled three or four at a time, backing into the library, trying to protect Simon from the onslaught. But I couldn't defend him and help Bennett at the same time. Simon wasn't strong enough, and I told him to forgive me as I left him to fend for himself—knowing he'd eventually be possessed.

Instead, I followed Bennett to the gallery, where Rachel knelt, opening the box of ashes at Neos's feet. Neos stood there watching with a distant superiority. The sight of him filled me with dread: that ancient, repulsive old ghost with his white scraggly hair and black crow-eyes, secure in his victory, more powerful than ever.

Neos twitched his fingers, and a claw of darkness slashed at Bennett, causing his dispelling spears to veer off at crazy angles. Bennett gasped in pain and struck again, but despite all his power, he couldn't hit Neos, not even a glancing blow. When I finally reached him, I didn't even know how he was still standing. Bloody and wounded, his blue eyes were fierce, bright and furious.

Until they flickered toward me for the briefest

moment, and I saw myself in them. He still loved me. In the middle of all this, he loved me. And I loved him and would protect him, no matter what the cost.

"This time," I told Neos, "you're not getting away."

"This time," he said, in his hissing voice, "I won't need to."

Instead of answering, I threw open the gates of my power.

This man—not "man," this *thing*—had haunted me. He'd torn my family apart, he'd ruined minds and lives. He'd killed Coby, Martha, Bennett's sister, and a dozen other ghostkeepers, and was damn near to killing Bennett, too.

Let's just say I didn't need to dig too deep to tap into all that rage.

And I had plenty.

I unleashed it at Neos—all of it.

The blast struck him in the center of his chest, and he stepped backward to keep from falling, the smug expression dropping from his face. I poured more and more power into him, so much that just the reflection of the attack dispelled ghosts on the library floor one story below.

But while the onslaught rocked Neos back a few steps, he didn't fall—he didn't even begin to unravel. I couldn't dispel him. Because something was protecting him, keeping my power from truly touching him.

He raised his left hand to me, and there, embedded in his palm, was my ring. Emma's ring. Blocking the power I blasted at him.

"Yes," Neos said, his smug look returning. "That is why I needed her ring. Like a vaccination, it lets me resist your particular brand of power. You're finished, Emma."

"She hasn't even started yet," Bennett snarled, and the spears of light flickered to life in his hands. "Together now."

He slashed at Neos while I shot ribbons of power around him. Something jumped me from behind and slammed me to my knees, but I didn't stop attacking. I heard Bennett gasp and saw his final spears blurring through the air, until I felt him falter a moment later.

That's when Neos said, "*Now*, Rachel."

Still kneeling at the box of ashes, she scattered them at Neos's feet, and I immediately felt the change. He absorbed them, drawing the ashes—the tiny traces of the living man he'd once been—into his spectral self.

Before our eyes, he morphed into a creature more monstrous than ever.

Flaps of skin peeled from him, his body shedding inky tentacles as he thickened and broadened. The tentacles resolved into smoky ropes, twisting and writhing.

Snakes. Dozens of snakes, made of smoke and ash, each of them wraithlike, slithering from his body to sway and snap in the air.

Like my vision. Like the tapestry at the Knell—showing my ancestor battling a ghostly snake—and my dream, back in San Francisco, of a ghost formed of snakes rising from my father's urns. Neos was my nightmare come to life. And too powerful, now, even with me and Bennett fighting together.

"Yes," he said, as if he could read my mind. "Now I only lack one thing. Your body."

A snake slithered through the air and wound around Rachel's shoulders—then sunk its fangs into her neck. She cried out, but didn't make a move to dislodge it. She just swayed there, her ghostly face contorted with pain, giving everything for what she imagined was love.

Until, a moment later, she shriveled like a raisin and crumpled to dust, the essence of her dead self swallowed by the snake to feed Neos.

"Now your turn," he said to Bennett. "Take Emma's power. Isn't that what you want?"

Bennett slashed at him, and was slammed into the wall by one of the ghastly snakes.

"Take her power, boy," Neos whispered. "Then see if you can beat me."

There was no other way. We couldn't beat him alone, and we couldn't beat him together. It felt like the inevitable conclusion to my vision. "Do it," I told Bennett.

"Yes," Neos hissed. "Listen to the girl. A woman in love will give you anything you ask."

Voices sounded from behind us, and for a moment I felt a desperate flash of hope. Then I saw that while my power had dispelled the possessions, freeing Max, Natalie, Lukas, and the others, they were now corralled in the lower floor of the library, guarded by wraiths. They watched, exhausted and weak, along with Coby, who'd made it back from the Beyond, but was powerless to help. Sara, Harry, and my parents had been discovered and stood there terrified, ringed by slavering wraiths who only awaited their master's word to feast.

"You've trained in the art of Asarum," Neos sneered at Bennett. "Hasn't that been your plan? Drain the most powerful ghostkeeper in centuries and *then* see if you can dispel me?"

"It's our only chance," I pleaded with him. "Do it, Bennett. I want you to."

Bennett wiped blood from his mouth. "He knows I can't win, Emma. He wants me to weaken you so—"

A snake shot forward and sank its fangs into my shoulder. Poison pumped into my flesh and I screamed. Distantly I heard Neos mocking Bennett, saying something about protecting me, saying that the only way to save me was to drain me dry.

I summoned my power through the red haze of agony, but with the ring protecting him, I couldn't make Neos stop. I couldn't think, I couldn't plan, I couldn't even see straight. But I did see *something*. Through tears of pain I saw Bennett's blue eyes, close to mine, as he took my hand.

He looked at me and said, "Everything I have is yours."

And he opened the floodgates. The principle of reflexivity meant that the ability to steal power was the same as the ability to give it away, and Bennett poured his power into me like a river pouring over a waterfall.

That had been his plan all along—not to drain my energy to fight Neos himself, but to give me the power to beat him.

I saw everything in that one moment. He'd been

afraid that I'd need to drain him dry, and that I would refuse to do it. He'd thought I might need to kill him to save us all—like the Rake had killed the original Emma to save her—and I wouldn't be able to do it.

So he gave me no choice. He kept his secret, he hoarded his power—and then he gave it all to me, without asking my permission. I was going to have some words with him later.

But right then?

I'd never felt power like that. All my powers—communicating, reading, summoning, dispelling, compelling—merged into a single power. I knew the story of every book and antique in that room; I felt the original Emma standing beside me, and the Emma before her, and the one before her. And I saw that I wasn't forced to follow my destiny; I was free to lead my destiny wherever I chose.

Lifetimes passed in the blink of two blue eyes, and I raised my head, looked at Neos, and said, "I told you I'd make you pay."

A bright white light coursed through my shoulder, into the snake's fangs and down its serpentine body to explode against Neos. He shrieked in pain and surprise, and sent an urgent message to his wraiths: *feed*.

Hoping to distract me. Hoping to give himself time to run.

I didn't look away from him as he crawled frantically toward the shadows. The wraiths howled and shuddered, and I turned them to smoke with a thought. Then I sent my power to cleanse the entire room—then the hallway—then the school and grounds.

Neos scuttled back until he hit the wall, then raised a hand in supplication. "I can feel all your power. So brilliant and strong. Let me be your follower. Spare me," he begged.

"I'll spare you . . ."

His eyes widened with hope.

"The lingering, painful death you deserve."

I raised my hand, and Neos exploded into dust.

I woke in the hospital. My shoulder was bandaged under the hospital gown, and ached from the ghostly snakebite. That surge of power had exhausted me after it burned out, leaving me weak and spent, and I'd collapsed to the floor.

I rolled to my side and saw Bennett sitting in the chair beside the bed, his hand inches from mine. I felt myself smile, as my fingers interlaced with his—with his beautiful, unstained hands. The red rings had already faded from his cobalt eyes, the purple blotches gone from his fingers.

I felt like I'd been dragged around behind a car like tin cans to celebrate someone's wedding—but despite the aches, my smile widened. Tears welled in my eyes. We'd done it. We'd won. Neos was gone, the dead were laid to rest. The nightmare was over, and our future had finally begun.

Bennett kissed my hand, and I touched the stubble on his cheek. He looked better than he had in months: strong, steady, and stable.

"You're still too skinny," I told him.

He laughed with easy pleasure, a sound I hadn't heard in months, and the tears of happiness welled in my eyes again.

"The Asarum is gone?" I asked.

"How much do you remember?" he asked. "I mean, after you dispelled Neos, but before you fainted?"

I furrowed my brow. "I remember I felt them—the other Emmas—and I saw the Beyond all around me. I saw the trapped souls, and the people who'd been possessed, and I—"

"You freed them. You fixed them—you healed the damage of the possessions, too. Everyone's fine."

"And *you*?"

He showed me his unstained fingers. "When you took my power, you took my addiction, too. You burned the Asarum out of me."

"I didn't *take* your power, you *gave* it. It worked, but . . . can you still see ghosts?"

He shook his head. "Not since that night. My powers are gone."

"Oh, Bennett." I squeezed his hand.

"I'm not sorry," he said. "I did what I needed to, and I—"

"You didn't need to die," I said, knowing now that's what he'd planned.

"I thought Neos would either kill you and me, and everyone we loved, or . . . it could just be me."

"How could you do that? Put me in the position where'd I'd be the one who—" I swallowed back tears.

"You'd have done exactly the same to me."

I opened my mouth to object—but didn't say anything. He was right. If I'd needed to surrender everything for him and my friends, I'd have done it. "Maybe," I finally said. "But at least *I'd* have the grace to feel guilty about it!"

"I don't regret anything. It's over, Em." His eyes burned into mine with their intense blueness. "I've got everything I want right here."

I still worried about him missing his ghostkeeping powers, but was more concerned with touching him, smelling him, now that he didn't reek of Asarum. I hitched myself higher in bed to kiss him, then winced at a sudden pang in my shoulder. "Ouch."

Bennett helped me lie back down. "You healed everyone except yourself. I've got something for you, but it can wait. Go back to sleep, and—"

And my family bustled into the room. "Oh, thank God!" my mom said, looking at me.

"Told you she'd be all right," Dad said. "She's a Vaile, isn't she?"

"Well, *something's* wrong," Max said, his brow knit with concern. "After twenty minutes alone with Bennett, she's still wearing her shirt."

"Jerk," I muttered, but I couldn't help smiling. Especially after Max and Bennett headed off together, giving my parents some time alone with me. I didn't want alone time with my parents so much, but was glad Max and Bennett seemed on the way to rebuilding their friendship.

My dad fluttered around, making sure I was

comfortable, while my mother peppered me with questions and news.

The Knell had their contacts in the police cover up the possessions at Thatcher by saying there was a gas leak that caused mass fainting, headaches, and temporary amnesia. And my mysterious wound? Well, I'd been treated for snakebite, and a ghostkeeper at Boston animal control claimed to have confiscated someone's missing pet python.

As my mom helped me dress to leave the hospital, I said, "So how bad's my shoulder?"

"Pretty bad," my dad said. "They said to expect a few months of bandages, physical therapy, and some scarring."

"How bad a scar?"

My mother burst into tears. "It's all my fault. Neos went insane because of me, and look what happened to poor Rachel. And now you're disfigured."

"Disfigured? Not helping, Mom." But I soothed her until she calmed down, telling her that none of this was her fault. "Neos was sick from the start. He didn't go insane because of you."

She sniffled. "Really?" She sat on the bed and wiped her eyes on the sleeve of her thick black wool sweater. "We still haven't been the best parents. We never should've kept your abilities from you."

Dad plopped down beside her. "We made a huge mistake there."

I nodded. "You did. But as much as I'd like to blame you for everything that's wrong in my life . . . I think I'm okay. I mean, I want everyone back. All those pointless deaths. I really miss Martha. And Coby . . ." Well, that was still unfinished business. "But I know who I am now. Who I want to be. I guess that makes you not the worst parents to ever walk the earth."

Dad smiled. "We'll take it."

My mom laid a hand on his knee. "There's something else we need to discuss, Emma. We're selling the house and business in San Francisco and going to work for the Knell full-time."

"We want you to come with us," Dad said.

My stomach dropped. How could I be so far away from Bennett? He'd be going back to Harvard. And what about my friends?

Mom saw my face and sighed. "The Sterns want you to stay with them, and finish the year at Thatcher."

Hope bloomed in my chest. "And after that?"

"We'd like you to spend some of the summer with us," Dad said, "but you can do your senior year at Thatcher."

"Thank you!" I beamed.

"You don't have to look so happy about it," my mother said.

I hugged her. "I love you guys."

And my mother started crying again. But this time she said they were good tears.

When I got home, everyone was waiting in the kitchen. Lukas was helping Harry flirt with a blushing Celeste, who he couldn't even see, as Coby and Sara watched in amusement. And Natalie and her mother were at the counter, stirring bowls of what looked like chocolate batter, under the watchful gaze of Anatole.

Simon and the Sterns saw me first, and stood to greet me. Everyone hugged me, then I sat in the nook next to Bennett. He seemed a little quiet; I worried it was because he couldn't see Anatole and Celeste. But he also seemed more like himself than he had for months. I cuddled against him, enjoying his warmth, as my friends teased me.

"Emma's so kick-ass," Harry said. "Did you see her open that can of exorcist on his ass?"

"I still say she needs a tramp stamp," Lukas said.

My mother glared at him.

"Maybe a delicate little snake on the inside of her wrist," Sara suggested.

"Emma would never get a tattoo," my mother declared.

I almost giggled, remembering my plan to secretly get inked when she and my dad had first disappeared. Hard to believe a tattoo had seemed the riskiest thing I could do at the time.

"How about some fierce piercings?" Natalie asked, licking batter from her spoon.

"Natalie!" her mother said, and they both smiled.

"Did you hear I got suspended?" Harry asked gleefully. "I am *persona non grata* at Thatcher for the next two weeks."

"For what?" I asked.

Sara giggled. "They suspect it wasn't a gas leak, and he dosed the lemonade."

"But he's sober!" I said.

He's still Harry, Coby told me with a grin.

Good point. I looked at Harry and asked, "Did you tell them it wasn't you?"

Harry drew himself up in mock offense. "I explained I had no idea what had happened. I was just trying to find my chimp."

"Your *chimp*?" Bennett asked with a half laugh.

"Despite what you might think, that is *not* a term of endearment for your girlfriend!" Harry explained, raising his hands in a placating gesture. "Even though she has monkey toes."

I ignored him as Bennett put his arm around my waist and whispered something sweet into my ear. I half listened to Sara telling a story about Harry's youthful fascination with Curious George, as Simon related some obscure point about spectral reading to Mr. Stern and my mom. Natalie opened the oven, then looked around for oven mitts, and my dad offered her his ghostly boxing gloves. She put them on and struck a boxing pose, and the smell of brownies and happy conversation filled the air.

And leaning against Bennett, still weak from my wound and exhausted from the fight, the truth sank in all over again. The long battle was finished, and we'd won. Everything that had happened with Neos, from my childhood on, was in the past, and *this* was the future. These people in this kitchen.

I knew who I was now, and where I was meant to be.

Were there still some questions? Sure, a few. But one thing I knew for certain:

I'd come home.

The first day of February was bitingly cold, but the sky was cloudless and picture-book blue. I was feeling stronger, walking with Bennett, Natalie, and Lukas from the museum to Echo Point Cemetery.

"This is a weird day to say good-bye," I said, looking at the sky. "We should wait for a cold, gray, drizzly day. How long before it rains again?"

"Emma," Natalie said gently. "This is what Coby wants."

Bennett clasped my mittened hand, and despite my mood I felt the pleasure of holding his hand without worrying about our power. He'd even put on a little weight since he'd been home—Anatole and Celeste had seen to that. But it wasn't enough to stop me from feeling sick over what we were about to do.

"You're not taking something from him," Bennett told me. "You're giving him what he wants."

"Still sucks, though," Lukas said.

Natalie glared at him. "Lukas, not helping."

"No, he's right," I agreed. "Why should I pretend it doesn't suck?"

"Because," Natalie answered, "that's how you get over the grieving." I guess she knew something about that. She was still hurting over losing Lukas—and having me and

Bennett together couldn't be making that easier. Even worse, her mother had gone back to the Kingdomers, though Mrs. Stern suspected she'd return to Echo Point soon.

We walked in silence the rest of the way. When we made the final turn, we could see Sara and Harry through the black iron gates, passing a coffee thermos back and forth as Coby messed with them—pulling Harry's cap down, playing with Sara's hair, grabbing the thermos and taking a sip of coffee that poured right through him and splashed on the ground—as though he wanted one final playful moment with them before he went. That's how they all must've looked when they were twelve.

We stopped outside the cemetery entrance, giving them some time.

"I can't do it," I suddenly said. "I can't."

Bennett pulled me close. "You have to let him go, Em."

I buried my face in his navy wool coat, quietly sobbing. He was right. I'd asked too much of Coby already. In the short time I'd known him, he'd been such a good friend to me, and all I'd done was use him. I owed this to him, no matter how much it hurt.

Bennett kissed the top of my head, and after I pulled myself together, I led him through the gates. Time to help one of my best friends find his peace.

When we got to the gravesite, I saw what Sara was wearing. All black, of course—but under her open coat was a little black dress, more appropriate for a party than a burial.

"I know," she said, seeing my expression. "I'm *freezing*."

"Then why that?" Natalie gestured toward the tiny dress.

"I woke up this morning," Sara said, "and he'd laid it out for me, on the foot of my bed."

"Really?" Natalie said. "That doesn't seem like him."

"I know. I just thought, well, if he's got one last request . . ." Sara's voice trailed off as she suddenly eyed Harry suspiciously. "Wait a minute. It *doesn't* sound like Coby."

"What?" Harry said, trying to look innocent.

"You snuck into my room last night!"

He laughed. "You're just lucky I couldn't find a bikini!" He raised the thermos and toasted the empty space beside him, where he must've thought Coby was standing. "One last prank, Coby, for you. Damn, I'm going to miss—" And he suddenly choked up, for once unable to find the words to say.

I turned to Coby. He wasn't standing beside Harry, he was stretched out on his own grave, still wearing the dark gray suit he'd worn to Homecoming.

Poor Harry, he said.

What are you doing down there? I asked.

He grinned. *Practicing.*

I couldn't help smiling at his macabre attitude. *And how does it feel?*

Cold and hard.

You can always change your mind, I said hopefully.

He stood. *No, I'm ready.*

Are you sure?

You gave me a gift, Coby said. *Being able to say a long good-bye like this—but it's time. Only, will you touch me again, so they can see me?*

You don't need my help. I remembered the Rake showing himself to Mr. Stern. *Just focus, and they'll see you. Do you want me to say anything to them?*

You can tell Sara I like the dress. Otherwise . . . He shook his head. *They know.*

He concentrated, and a point of light started in his chest and expanded into a glowing aura. He stepped in front of Harry and Sara, and he was right—he didn't need words.

"You gorgeous bastard," Harry said. "I'll never forget you."

Sara didn't say anything, she just began to weep. My heart ached for them. It was like he was dying a second time.

I did something I hadn't planned. I stepped close to him and stood on my tiptoes and kissed him. A sweet, simple good-bye kiss on the lips that made my mouth tingle from ghostbite.

Then I said, *I could've loved you, Coby.*

Yeah, Emma. He smiled at me. *Maybe next lifetime.*

I'll see you then, I said, and dispelled him, turning him to dust.

The wind blew drifts of snow around, and the few dead

leaves still clinging to the trees fluttered and shook. Coby's ashes mingled with it all. But spring would come. Somewhere beneath the cold earth, life bided its time. And maybe Coby and I would see each other again one day.

"He's gone," Sara said. "I can feel it. This time for good."

Natalie hugged her, and she started to sob. Then Harry shattered the silence with a pained yell, hurling his thermos into the woods. With tears in his eyes, he said, "I want a drink."

I hugged him fiercely. "It'll have to be one of my special chais, Harry. Have I made you a dirty one yet?"

"I want mine filthy," he said.

We trudged back to the museum together, and toasted Coby with dirty vanilla chai lattes.

That evening, I slipped into black leggings and my long gray sweater and went to find the Rake. I took a rapier from Mr. Stern's study, and expected the Rake to appear in the ballroom the moment I stepped through the doors, but the room remained quiet.

Until Bennett spoke from the doorway. "Do you remember that night we flashed back?"

I turned and smiled. "Only every single detail."

He crossed toward me, a grin curving his mouth—then he stopped. "Should I get the other blade?"

I looked at the sword in my hand. "I'm waiting for the Rake."

He raised a brow. "The *Rake*?"

Oh, right, we'd never talked about him. "He's a ghost. Your ancestor. The Bennett you're named after."

"What?" Bennett laughed in surprise. "Here? When did he show up?"

"Um . . . a couple days after you brought me here from San Francisco."

"Why didn't you tell me?"

"He's private. And you're both Bennetts. It'd be like . . . I don't know. Traveling back in time and meeting yourself."

"And you call him 'the Rake'?"

"Well, he's all swagger and devilish charm," I explained.

"In that case, how can you tell us apart?"

I pressed closer to him. "Actually, now that you say that . . . he's also incredibly loyal and tough and loved Emma." I told him the Rake's story, finishing with, ". . . and so he killed her, to save her. And he's never left."

"I wouldn't leave, either," Bennett said. "Wait, that reminds me—everything's been so crazy, I forgot to give you this." He reached into his pocket and gave me Emma's ring. "I grabbed it after you dispelled Neos."

I ran my finger along the curve of the ring. "It's weird, but it kind of doesn't feel like it's mine anymore."

Perhaps it is not, the Rake said, materializing near the piano.

Oh! I spun, smiling in happy surprise. *There you are!*

"Is he here?" Bennett asked.

"Yeah, he just came."

The Rake swept me with one of his arrogant looks. *Why don't you let me speak to him myself?*

He can't even see you, not anymore. I still wasn't sure how we were going to deal with this.

Emma, he said, *Bennett gave you his power. Including his ability to take power—or grant it.*

"Omigod," I said, realizing.

"What?" Bennett asked. "You know, I never realized how annoying it is when ghostkeepers talk to people you can't see!"

"Well," I smiled, "don't get used to it."

I took his hand and pushed power into him. There was some resistance, but I felt a trickle of ghostkeeping energy swirl between us, and he said, "Whoa! I can see him. I—I can barely feel the energy, and it's . . . different."

It will take some time, the Rake told him. *And you will never be the same as you were.*

Holy sh—I can hear you! Bennett said. *I can communicate.*

You have Emma's powers—just less so. The Rake considered him closely, his eyes hooded. *I heard what happened. That you forced Emma to take your powers.*

It was the only way to save her, Bennett said, apparently willing to confide in this previous version of himself. *Would you not have done the same?*

The Rake smiled suddenly. *I think this is what I've been waiting for. I loved my Emma, but you—did better. Now I can go. And perhaps even . . .*

Be with her? I asked.

Perhaps, the Rake said. *May I have the ring?*

I opened my palm, and his ghostly fingers plucked the ring away. He looked at me for a long moment, then Bennett. Then his hand shimmered and glowed, as power from the ring started to spread through him—not quite a dispelling, but close.

I expected some final words from him, but instead he addressed Bennett. *I don't think it's easy for them to love us. On the other hand . . .*

Then the Rake bowed to me one final time and disappeared forever.

Too much. First Coby, then this. I broke into tears again, and only after he'd comforted me did I ask Bennett, "On the other hand?"

"What?"

"The Rake said it's not easy for us to love you—which isn't true, by the way—but on the other hand . . . what?"

"Ah." Bennett kissed me until I forgot everything but the shape of his mouth and the taste of his lips. Then he drew back and said, "On the other hand, we love you forever."

ACKNOWLEDGMENTS

I am ever grateful to the wonderful Nancy Coffey, Joanna Volpe, and Kathleen Ortiz. My excellent editor, Caroline Abbey, always seemed to know the books better than I did, and my publicists, Deb Shapiro and Kate Lied, have been the best. I also had incredibly supportive writer friends, Melissa Senate and Lisa and Laura Roecker. Thank you, one and all.

Lee Nichols is the author of the Haunting Emma trilogy. She was raised in Santa Barbara, California—the setting of her adult novels *Tales of a Drama Queen*, *Hand-Me-Down*, and *True Lies of a Drama Queen*. She attended Hampshire College in Amherst, Massachusetts, where she studied history and psychology. She now lives in Maine and is married to novelist Joel Naftali.

www.leenicholsbooks.com